JUL 0 9 1003

WHAT ARE WE GOING TO DO ABOUT

DAVID?

Books By
WILLO DAVIS ROBERTS

The View from the Cherry Tree
Don't Hurt Laurie
The Minden Curse
More Minden Curses
The Girl with the Silver Eyes
The Pet-sitting Peril
Baby-sitting Is a Dangerous Job
No Monsters in the Closet
Eddie and the Fairy Godpuppy
The Magic Book
Sugar Isn't Everything
Megan's Island
What Could Go Wrong?
Nightmare
To Grandmother's House We Go
Scared Stiff
Jo and the Bandit
What Are We Going to Do about David?

WHAT ARE WE GOING TO DO ABOUT

DAVID?

WILLO DAVIS ROBERTS

A Jean Karl Book

Atheneum 1993 New York

Maxwell Macmillan Canada
Toronto

Maxwell Macmillan International
New York Oxford Singapore Sydney

Atheneum
Macmillan Publishing Company
866 Third Avenue
New York, NY 10022

Maxwell Macmillan Canada, Inc.
1200 Eglinton Avenue East
Suite 200
Don Mills, Ontario M3C 3N1

Macmillan Publishing Company is part of the Maxwell Communication Group of
Companies.

First edition
Printed in the United States of America
10 9 8 7 6 5 4 3 2 1
The text of this book is set in 12 point Electra.
Book design by Tania Garcia

Library of Congress Cataloging-in-Publication Data

Roberts, Willo Davis.
    What are we going to do about David? / Willo Davis Roberts.—1st ed.
        p.   cm.
    "A Jean Karl book."
    Summary: Upset that his parents do not seem to pay any attention to him or
care about him, eleven-year-old David becomes even more worried when they
deposit him for the summer with a grandmother he hardly knows so that they
can go about their own busy lives.
    ISBN 0-689-31793-X
    [1. Parent and child—Fiction.   2. Grandmothers—Fiction.]
I. Title.
PZ7.R54465We   1993
[Fic]—dc20   92-4726

To the children in Texas and Ohio
who suggested this book

—WDR

WHAT ARE WE GOING TO DO ABOUT

DAVID?

I knew I was in trouble the minute I saw Mom's car parked in front of our apartment house.

I swallowed hard, remembering now, too late, that I had been instructed to come straight home from school today instead of going to Tim's house the way I usually did.

Normally Mom wouldn't have been home this time of afternoon. She would have been at her real estate office. But today Dad was coming home from New Jersey, and I was supposed to have been home by four o'clock to go with Mom to the airport to meet him.

I looked at the new watch Grandma Elsie had given me for my eleventh birthday only a month ago. I was over half an hour late.

The books and papers, including the yellow-covered copy of the school magazine, started to slip out of my hands, and I caught them just in time. I began to run.

I dropped the *Evergreen* once and made a little tear in the cover. The magazine contained the stories and poems of everyone in the school who had been chosen by their teachers to be published. Each class had a limited amount of space, and many of the students who had tried out weren't chosen to be included.

I was proud that my poem was one of the winners, but I had mixed feelings about showing it to my parents. On one hand, I hoped they'd be proud of me, the way they would have been if I'd brought home a soccer trophy for best player or something. On the other, I was nervous about showing my private feelings. Except to my friend Tim, I wasn't used to doing that.

Now wouldn't be a good time to share the poem, though. Not when Mom was probably mad at me for being late.

I got a better grip on the magazine and my notebook and hurried up the walk, stepping aside when the front doors opened and Consuela burst through them.

Consuela had worked for us for six months now, and I liked her a lot. She was not only a great cook, but she *talked* to me, as if I were a grown-up. She was also very pretty to look at for a woman her age, older than my mom.

She was crying. I'd never seen her cry. Her face was red, and she didn't notice me until I spoke to her.

She stopped, blew her nose, and stared down at me. She was only a little bit taller than I was.

"David. Your mother is mad that you're late."

"I forgot we had to go to Sea-Tac after Dad," I confessed. "What's the matter? Why are you crying?"

Beyond Consuela in the lobby, behind the glass doors, Mom was getting off the elevator, so I talked fast. "What's happened?" I demanded.

"Your mother just fired me," Consuela said. Her dark eyes flashed with anger. "She told me to get out and said she'd mail my final check."

That was all there was time for before my mother came practically boiling out the front door. "David, you're late, and your father is going to be livid if he's left standing around the airport. Come on, get in the car."

Though her tone was angry, I scarcely heard her. "But why?" I asked Consuela.

Her mascara had made dark smudges around her eyes. "Because for once I spoke my mind. I'm sorry, David. I'm going to miss you."

"David, there is no time for this." Mom took my arm and steered me toward the car, but I hung back, not believing that this could happen. "Mom, you can't fire Consuela! Mom, please!"

Her mouth set in a straight line, the way it did when she and Dad disagreed about anything. She tugged at my arm. "Don't make me any more irritated than I already am. I have let her go, and there is nothing to discuss. *Get in the car immediately!*"

There was nothing to do but go. Consuela, behind us, spoke loudly. "If it hadn't been for David, I wouldn't have worked for you past the first week, Mrs. Madison.

You are a vain, selfish, disagreeable, and demanding woman. And you know nothing about raising a child. I feel very sorry for your son." She hesitated before adding, "And your husband too."

I gulped. I'd never heard anybody speak to my mother that way before.

Most people thought Mom was clever and beautiful. She was slim and blond, like me, and was usually calm and cool. Right this minute she was so angry that she didn't seem pretty at all. It made me feel strange and uncomfortable.

She didn't answer Consuela. She jerked open the door of the maroon Chrysler and shoved me into the front seat so hard I clipped my head, but she didn't notice when I yelped in pain. Either that, or she didn't care. By the time she slid under the wheel on the other side, I was rubbing my head, and my eyes were watering. Consuela came to stand beside the car. There were tears in her eyes.

"Good-bye, David," she said. "Be a good boy! Take care of yourself!"

I turned to look back at her as we pulled away from the curb, too upset to return her wave. I fastened my seat belt automatically, biting my lip. I wanted to know what had happened, but this didn't seem like a good time to ask.

Mom's cheeks were still hot and red when we climbed the ramp to I-5 and headed south. She drove several miles along the freeway before she spoke. "I specifically reminded you this morning that Dad was coming home today. That you were not to stop at Tim's on the way home."

My voice was small. "I'm sorry. I forgot. Tim got a new Nintendo, and we were going to play—"

"You can explain that to your father when he wants to know why we're late." She pulled out to pass a truck. "What is it going to take for you to develop a sense of responsibility, David? You're old enough to do a simple thing like coming directly home after school."

I could only remember a few times in my whole life when it had made any difference. I slouched miserably in the seat, rubbing my head where it still hurt. "I just . . . forgot."

Usually there was no hurry about coming home. Nobody was ever there except on Tuesdays and Fridays when Consuela was busy with the vacuuming and cleaning. While she folded laundry or stirred or chopped things in the kitchen, I could sit on a stool at the counter and we'd talk. Sometimes she had baked cookies, the thick, chewy ones I especially liked, or maybe she'd set out a bowl of big red apples, and we ate while we talked.

I liked talking to Consuela. My parents prided themselves on being modern and broad-minded, but they often evaded the subject I wanted to discuss or said we'd talk about it later when Dad wasn't late getting to a meeting or Mom didn't have an appointment with a client to show a property. Consuela would talk about anything, no matter what else she was doing. Trouble at school, why it was stupid to do drugs, how unfair life could be when a bigger kid like Burt Talbot picked on me, what it was like to be lonely. Sometimes we quoted poetry to each other.

Mom once remarked that Consuela was ignorant because she only went to the ninth grade in school, but Consuela knew a lot of things. She read books and listened to talk shows, and she liked poetry. I'd learned some of the poems she knew, and we'd chant them together. Things with words like, "Out of the night that covers me, / dark as the pit from pole to pole, / I thank whatever gods may be / for my unconquerable soul."

I sure didn't have an unconquerable soul, but it seemed like a nice idea. Sometimes, like now, my soul felt pretty much squashed.

Consuela was the only one I'd told in advance about getting my poem published in the *Evergreen*. I'd looked forward to sharing it with Consuela, and now she was gone. After what she'd said to Mom, I couldn't imagine that she'd ever be hired back.

I glanced at Mom's profile, carefully, so she wouldn't notice and speak to me again. I repeated the words in my head. Vain, Consuela had called her. Selfish, disagreeable, and demanding. It made my face feel hot, thinking about it. Not even Dad, when they were having a disagreement about something, had ever said anything like that to Mom. It was no wonder Consuela had been fired.

Yet Consuela had always been friendly and helpful,

even with math homework or skinned elbows. She never tattled on me for anything, though she made me keep the rules Mom had laid down.

You don't know anything about raising children. I feel sorry for your son. What had she meant? Had they quarreled over *me*?

Was it somehow *my* fault that Consuela had been fired?

The idea that something I'd said or done might have hurt Consuela made me feel awful. Consuela's husband, Arturo, drove a cab, and he didn't make enough money to support the four kids they still had at home. Consuela needed the money she'd earned working for us. She'd have a hard time getting another job if she admitted she'd been fired from her last one.

I'd miss her a lot. I swallowed hard and wondered what Mom had said to make Consuela so rude that Mom had fired her. It must have had something to do with *me* or Consuela would never have said, "You don't know anything about raising children."

What, though?

Mom did have different ideas about raising children than Tim's mother. Mrs. Patton was pretty laid back. She didn't care if Tim didn't keep his room neat all the time, the way I was expected to do. She just said, "If you aren't going to clean up that mess, keep your door closed so the rest of us don't have to look at it." She let her kids get into the refrigerator whenever they were hungry; and when we wanted to set up electric trains all over the living room, Tim's mom didn't object as long as we put everything away before I went home.

Mom said she couldn't allow us to make a mess in *our* living room because either she or Dad might have a client drop in. My bedroom wasn't big enough for the whole layout when we put all our trains and equipment together. That was why I'd hauled most of my stuff over to Tim's and left it there, and why I almost always went home with Tim after school.

I had the best trains and the most tracks. But Tim had a whole village with a sawmill with moving saws; a church with a steeple and a real bell; a miniature carnival, on the edge of the little town, with a carousel and a Ferris wheel that really turned. For the past week we'd been building a waterwheel that worked on a battery on the plastic river. We'd tried to figure out a way to have real water in the river instead of blue plastic, but even Tim's mom vetoed every way we could think of to do it.

Tim and I spent hours cutting and shaping and gluing, and Mrs. Patton never complained about the smell or the shavings we got on the carpet, or about having another boy around when she already had two of her own.

Did that mean she was a better mother? She wore jeans and sweatshirts and moccasins rather than dresses or suits with nylons and high heels, and she kept her hair cut short and straight instead of going to the beauty parlor every week for a shampoo and set the way Mom did. She didn't work at a regular job, but she did a lot of volunteer work at the hospital, so she wasn't always home either. But she sure was different from Mom.

Was there really something wrong with my own mother?

I was confused enough that I didn't notice the siren behind us until Mom swore under her breath and touched the brakes, easing toward the side of the freeway.

I bit my lip as the car rolled to a stop. Mom pushed the button that lowered the window beside her. Her knuckles were white where she clenched them on the steering wheel as the uniformed state patrol officer bent his head to see in the window.

"Good afternoon, ma'am. May I see your driver's license and registration, please?"

The only time I'd ever been this close to a patrolman before was two years ago with Dad when we'd hit black ice. The car had slid into a ditch and rolled over. Even after I realized we weren't badly hurt, it was scary. I was sure relieved when the state patrol showed up to rescue us, because my door was under us and Dad's door was jammed shut so he couldn't open it. The officer had been very kind. He said that the cut on my head wasn't serious, and he handed me a teddy bear dressed in a blue state patrol uniform, wearing a badge. "Just hang on to this fella," the officer said.

It was kind of embarrassing to be given a teddy bear for comfort. I thought I probably ought to tell the officer that nine-year-olds were too big for teddy bears. But I couldn't quite get up the nerve to say so, and I took the bear home with me. I never played with it, of course, but it still sat on my dresser. I'd even given it a name: Officer McGoo.

I almost wished I had it now. This patrolman didn't seem nearly as friendly as that other one had been. In fact, his mouth looked flat and grim as Mom handed over her driver's license. Her hand was shaking.

"The registration form is in the glove compartment. Get it for me, please, David."

Mom's voice didn't sound normal. Nervously, I found the paper she'd asked for and passed it over so she could hand it to the police officer.

He compared Mom with the picture on her license, glanced keenly at me so that I felt like squirming. "I clocked you doing seventy-two miles an hour, ma'am."

There was a spot of pink in each of Mom's cheeks. "I'm sorry, officer. I was in a hurry—we're late to pick my husband up at Sea-Tac—"

The officer was unmoved. "And you're not wearing your seat belt, ma'am."

The pink spot got brighter. "I was in a hurry. I'm usually careful about buckling up, but this time I just forgot—"

She sounded angry. With me? I wondered. It was my fault we were late.

The officer said nothing more. He began to write out a ticket. I felt frozen and unhappy. Mom was bound to be in a rotten mood for the rest of the evening.

The officer handed her license and the registration

papers back; then he gave her the ticket. "Please fasten your seat belt now, ma'am," he said, and waited until she did it before he touched the brim of his hat and walked back to his own car.

Mom's teeth were clenched as she shifted into drive. "Your father is going to kill us," she said, easing back into traffic. "Can you finally see how inconsiderate you are when you don't obey orders?"

I huddled miserably in the seat and wondered how a day that had started out so great, when I got my poem published in the *Evergreen*, could now have gone so completely wrong. And it wasn't over yet. There was still my dad to face.

2

D ad traveled on business for the computer company where he worked as a junior vice president. He often flew to distant cities, usually for no more than a few days. This time he had been gone for a week.

Usually I enjoyed going to Sea-Tac, the big airport between Seattle and Tacoma. I liked the twisting spiral ramps that went around and around, climbing to different levels in the parking garage. The escalators that went deep underground to the little train that ran out to the North Satellite where we were to meet Dad's plane were kind of fun too.

It was impossible to enjoy anything today, though. The plane should have landed nearly an hour ago. Mom was still angry and upset enough so she'd hardly said a word to me since the cop had given her the ticket except to let me know how stupid I was. It hadn't helped that we got caught in heavy traffic either; it was practically gridlocked coming through Seattle.

The passengers from New Jersey had already left when we got to Dad's gate, and only a few people had gathered for the next flight out, which wasn't due for another hour.

I cleared my throat. "Maybe Dad took the Airporter."

The look Mom gave me made me wish I'd kept still.

"You'd better hope he didn't," she said. "He *hates* taking the Airporter. Why else would I drive all this way in rush-hour traffic?"

It seemed safer to keep still. I supposed it really was mostly *my* fault for making us late, but I couldn't help wishing that she'd stop reminding me.

I just forgot, I thought miserably. Everybody forgot things occasionally, didn't they? Dad had been known to forget his briefcase, Mom her keys or something in the oven. Why was it so much worse when *I* did it?

"He's probably picking up his luggage. I'd better have him paged, just to make sure he doesn't leave the terminal without us," Mom said, and left me standing there alone while she went to one of the white courtesy phones to take care of that.

When the announcement was made that Jerrol Madison was to call in, I hoped Dad heard it. It wasn't very loud, and there was quite a bit of other noise as a group of chattering tourists, speaking a language I couldn't understand, came along the corridor.

When the hand clamped down on my shoulder, I

jumped. "Oh, hi, Dad. We were afraid we'd missed you."

"What the heck happened to you? My plane got in a long time ago."

I licked my lips and took a deep breath. I might as well tell him before Mom did. "It was my fault. I forgot I was supposed to come home early."

"Then she should have left you at Tim's and come alone," Dad said. "Serve you right to go home to an empty apartment. It might help your memory next time." He didn't sound cross, though. He just looked very tired.

Mom was coming back from the telephone, but she wasn't smiling to see either one of us. Usually my parents kissed each other hello, but today they didn't even brush cheeks. Instead, Mom gave me a resentful stare and said, "I suppose David's already told you about the ticket."

I sucked in a painful breath. "No, I didn't," I began, but Dad spoke over my words.

"What ticket, Gail? Is that it?"

The corner of it was sticking out of the side pocket of her purse, and he reached out and took it. His tone was the one that always made me cringe.

"Speeding? Gail, for crying out loud, seventy-two miles an hour? And not wearing a seat belt? What's wrong with you?"

Mom was pale but defensive. "I've had a perfectly terrible day, Jerrol. I thought the sale of that Midland property was a sure thing, and at the last minute the client backed out. Then I had a very nasty scene with

Consuela and fired her, and to top it all off David was late—"

"To top it all off you drove too fast—with David in the car—and didn't have your seat belt fastened," Dad corrected, scowling at the ticket in his hand. "I thought we agreed, when David was just a baby, that we'd never speed and we'd always use seat belts, to set him a good example."

I hated it when my parents quarreled. They'd been doing it a lot lately. It was even worse when they argued about *me*. It made me feel awful, just the way I felt now. Some of the people heading for the departure gates were looking at us. I wanted to pretend that I didn't belong to these two adults who were glaring at each other.

"Why didn't you leave David behind if he didn't get home when he was supposed to? And is it his fault you were driving without a seat belt so you got soaked with an extra fine? For pete's sake, Gail, you're supposed to be the adult!"

Before she could respond, Dad realized what Mom had said to him a moment earlier, and his face darkened even further. "You fired Consuela? What on earth for?" He didn't give her a chance to answer. "You sound to me as if you've lost your mind. Come on, let's get out of here before I lose my temper in front of everybody in the place."

He turned and headed briskly toward the escalators, carrying his suitcase and walking fast as if trying to leave us behind.

I got the feeling neither of them even remembered me now. I had to trot to keep up with Dad's long strides, and Mom had trouble too in her high heels.

It was taken for granted that Dad would drive home. He always drove when all three of us went anywhere. And on the trip home I clutched the armrest and wished they would shut up instead of snarling at each other.

"Consuela, for pete's sake," Dad said. "The best housekeeper we've had in years! She's reliable, always shows up when she's supposed to, and gets the oven clean. She doesn't steal things out of the freezer or snoop in our dresser drawers. And the woman can actually cook! She likes David, he likes her. What were you thinking of?"

"If you'd heard the way she talked to me, you wouldn't blame me. She was insufferable, telling me what I was doing wrong about raising my own son!"

"And what are you doing wrong about David, outside of setting him a rotten example when you drive?" Dad asked dryly.

"Everything, according to Consuela! You're included too, so you needn't feel complacent. We don't spend enough time with him, we don't understand him, we give him too many material things and not enough attention—she went on and on. And she said I'm selfish and—"

Huddled in the backseat, I tried to make myself deaf. Neither of them spoke to me, but they were talking *about* me. Dad drove precisely at the speed limit, but it seemed to me we would never get home, that they'd never stop saying horrible things. I wished they wouldn't keep making me feel so guilty.

I squeezed my eyes closed and put my fingers in my ears, and couldn't wait until we were home so I could escape to my room. I closed the door on the angry words that seemed to have no end, and stared at Officer McGoo on the dresser, his police cap tilted to a jaunty angle. "You're supposed to be a comfort to me," I told him accusingly. "But you don't help a bit."

He simply stared at me with his black button eyes, and suddenly I felt like crying, just the way I had before the police officer rescued us from Dad's wrecked car.

It wasn't until Sunday that I brought out my copy of the *Evergreen* to show my parents the poem I'd had published.

They were still cool to each other all day Saturday. Since Consuela hadn't finished her last day's work, neither of the bathrooms had been cleaned. Mom suggested that I might clean them, but before I could protest, Dad intervened.

"You're the one who fired Consuela. Why punish anybody else? Besides, I told David we'd go over to the park and play a little catch when I got home."

I wasn't much more excited about that than I was about scrubbing the bathtub. I wasn't very good at either throwing or catching. But clearly Dad was in a better humor than Mom was, so I said nothing.

At least Dad didn't criticize when I missed a catch or didn't throw far enough or threw too far. I knew he would have liked nothing better than to have a jock for a son. Dad had been good at just about everything athletic when he was a kid. For a while he'd hoped to pitch for the U Dub, which was what they called the University of Washington where he was going to college. Then Grandpa Frank died, and there was no money to stay in school.

"But it's okay," Dad had assured me once when we'd been talking about it. "I guess it was a sort of juvenile dream, to play big-league ball some day. I discovered computers and I'm pretty well satisfied working with those. But if you have any aptitude for playing ball, son, I'll help you all I can."

It seemed to me that it must have been obvious from the time I was about six that I didn't have any aptitude for anything that took coordination. I tripped over things, fell down steps, tipped over and spilled and broke things. It annoyed Mom, but I didn't feel quite so bad when Dad said, "I was the same way when I was his age, Gail. He's just growing so fast he can't keep up with his hands and feet."

We'd practiced throwing and catching balls for years now, and I didn't see where I was getting any better. A part of me wanted to say, "Why don't we just forget it, Dad?" But another part enjoyed Dad's company and wanted to please him, so I kept on trying to act as if I enjoyed throwing balls back and forth.

Today, though, I didn't have to pretend for long. I threw high and wild, and when Dad backed up to try for it he collided with a stupid kid on a bike who plowed right into him.

They went down in a heap. The kid started to cry, his mother came and scolded him for being off the bike path, and Dad sat on the grass and peeled down his sock to examine a bloody gouge on his ankle.

I felt guilty that it wasn't my injury. It looked painful. "I guess we'd better go home and clean that up, huh, Dad?"

"Oh, I'll live. What do you say we go get a burger for lunch so we don't interrupt Mom's cleaning?"

We both knew Mom hated cleaning—it ruined her fingernails, which she was quite proud of—and she wouldn't be in a very good mood. So we went to McDonald's and then drove down by the marina and watched the boats go in and out for a while.

By this time I had figured out that Dad didn't want to go home anymore than I did. When we finally got there, though, the apartment was empty. The note on the refrigerator said, "The Midland deal is back on. Probably won't be home until late. Why don't you eat out?"

Dad grunted. "Why don't we rent a video and order in pizza, sport?"

It was a good movie, an adventure with plenty of suspense and comedy. I felt practically normal, and started to relax, but with a movie on, there was no conversation.

I took the last piece of pizza with me when I went to

bed. I put it down next to Mr. McGoo while I got un-
dressed. "Don't eat any of it," I warned him.

I felt silly talking to a teddy bear, but sometimes there
wasn't anyone else to talk to.

I heard Mom come home about ten minutes later.
She didn't look in on me, though I knew she could see
the light under my door. When I was a little kid she used
to sit on the edge of my bed every night and read me a
story, but she hadn't done that for a long time. I was old
enough to read my own stories.

I held my breath, waiting for the cross voices to re-
sume the argument. Instead, though I couldn't understand many of the words, I knew by her voice that Mom
had either closed one of her real estate deals or something
else good had happened. She sounded happy, and Dad
seemed to have mellowed out too.

Good. If they were okay tomorrow, I'd show them
the poem. I got out the *Evergreen* and reread it myself.
It felt strange, but nice, to see my own words printed out
on the page.

I wasn't quite ready to go to sleep yet, so I read a few
more things the other kids had written.

Tommy Slade had written a poem about how good
he was at swimming, better than anyone else. It was true
he was a good swimmer, but the poem was kind of stupid.
I wondered how it had been picked to be included.

I decided to read one more. On the next page was a
poem by Samantha Purtill. It was all about how she went

to her grandmother's for Thanksgiving, and all the food they had, and all the cousins and other relatives who were there.

It sounded great—the kind of thing I had always missed, because I didn't have any cousins, or even aunts and uncles, because each of my parents was an only child. All I had was Grandma Elsie and Grandma Ruthie, and on holidays we all went to a fancy restaurant for dinner. When I'd go to Tim's house the next day, we'd have leftover turkey sandwiches, and maybe cold stuffing with onions and sage. And there would be pumpkin pie, with real whipped cream. Tim's mom managed that kind of thing even though her volunteer work kept her almost as busy as my mom's job did.

I had hoped that this year Consuela might roast a turkey and make pies and maybe my grandmothers would come *here* for Thanksgiving. And then I would have leftovers, like everybody else.

Now, of course, it wouldn't happen. And it hadn't happened to Samantha that way, either. She had made the whole thing up, at least if she was talking about *last* year.

I knew because the day before Thanksgiving I had been to the supermarket to buy bread and I'd stood in line behind Samantha and her dad at the check-out counter.

Samantha had lived alone with him since her mother died when we were in the second grade. Some of the kids made fun of her because she got her clothes at Goodwill, but she always looked all right to me. I didn't know how they could tell. I think maybe the other girls were jealous because she was so smart and got As on practically every test except math.

Anyway, I'd seen what the Purtills had in their basket as they prepared for the holiday. Two turkey TV dinners and a can of cranberry sauce.

I sighed and closed the magazine. Tomorrow, I thought, I would show my poem to my parents. And if I was lucky, maybe they'd think it was as wonderful as *I* thought it was, to have something I had written published where other people could read it.

I closed the *Evergreen* and turned off the light.

3

It seemed a good time. Dad had finished the Sunday paper, and it was too early to turn on the TV for the ball game. My mouth felt dry when I brought out the *Evergreen* and carried it into the living room. "I've got something to show you," I said, handing it over.

Dad took the school magazine with the bright yellow cover. "What's this?"

"Page thirty-two," I told him. A little tingle of excitement began inside me. I had written poems and little stories for a long time, but I'd seldom shown them to anyone except Tim. Jake Vier found one in my desk, once, and read it aloud to some of the other kids, making it sound silly. So I'd been more careful about exposing any more of my private thoughts in front of people. When I had to write a story as a class assignment, I usually got an A. Once the teacher asked me to read it aloud to the rest of the kids, and nobody laughed that time. Still, I hadn't taken any more chances.

Dad looked up questioningly, then found page thirty-two. "Well, well. What's this? 'My Treasure Chest,' by David Madison."

He read it aloud.

My chest is like me,
My chest keeps quiet
Just like me.
My chest keeps to itself
Just like me.
My chest won't let anyone
See its feelings
Or its true self
Just like me.
My chest has made a wall around it
Just like me.
My chest won't open
Just like me.

Dad stopped reading and I held my breath. Would Dad understand what I was trying to say, or would he think the poem was stupid?

Dad looked up slowly and smiled. "You are a deep one, aren't you, David. My dad, Grandpa Frank, was like that. Kept what he thought and felt to himself most of the time. But once in a while he'd tell me something—about life, about how to handle the things that happened to me—and it would always be important. I think I still remember most of what he said. You're a lot like Grandpa Frank."

Relief and pleasure swept over me. "You loved Grandpa Frank, didn't you, Dad?"

Carefully, as if the magazine were important, Dad closed the pages and handed the *Evergreen* back to me. "I loved him very much," he agreed. "And I love you too son. I couldn't write a poem if my life depended on it." His grin was wry. "I can't write poems, and you have trouble catching balls, but we can each of us respect the other for trying, and for what we *are* good at. It's a good poem, David."

For some reason, my eyes prickled, as if I wanted to cry, even though I didn't feel bad at all.

"Only seven kids from my class had their poems picked to be in the magazine," I said. The pride I felt was justified now. I'd show it to Mom as soon as she came home. She'd had to run over to the office to finish up the paperwork she expected to be signed on Monday for the big sale she was finally going to close.

Dad was still smiling. "Congratulations," he said, and I felt good all over.

A few minutes later I heard the front door open. Now if only Mom was in a good mood too, I thought hopefully.

She was. She was laughing, kissed first Dad and then me, and then whirled in a circle before collapsing in a chair. "I did it! I sold that property, and it'll be the biggest commission I ever made! We weren't supposed to talk about it again until tomorrow, but I had this one little question, so I called the client, and he'd made up his mind! Wanted to know if he could come over to the office right away and sign, so of course I said yes!"

She laughed again, almost giddy with delight. "I wanted it so badly, and I thought I'd lost it, and now it's done! Closing in thirty days, and then I'll get a check big enough to—to do anything I like!"

"Congratulations," Dad said, laughing back. "You'd be easier to live with, lady, if you made a major sale about once a week."

"How about once a day?" she teased, and got up. "I stopped at the deli on the way home and picked up salads and cold cuts for when you're hungry."

This would be a good time, I decided. She was happy enough to have forgotten she'd been mad at me. When she finished putting away the stuff from the deli, I was waiting for her with my poem.

"I already showed it to Dad," I said. "Page thirty-two."

"The school magazine?" She seemed mystified. Sinking onto a kitchen chair she turned to the right page.

I watched her face as she read, trying to interpret her reaction.

"What's this?" she asked, though she'd surely had time to read it all the way through by now.

"It's a poem I wrote," I said uncertainly. "Only seven kids from my class had poems that were chosen."

"You wrote this? Well." She hesitated and my stomach began to form into a knot. "It doesn't rhyme," she pointed out.

"Mrs. Post says poems don't necessarily have to rhyme." I wished I hadn't shown it to her after all. It was like telling a joke to someone who doesn't get it.

"I always sort of liked the kind that rhymes," Mom said. "But I'm glad your teacher thought it was one of the better ones, that she picked it to be printed." She smiled, but it was too late.

I already knew she didn't really like it. She proved it by adding, "Could you explain what it means, exactly? I didn't know you had a treasure chest."

My mouth felt stiff. "If I have to explain, it doesn't mean anything," I managed to say, then took the magazine out of her hands and headed for my room.

"David! Honey, wait, I'm sorry, I didn't mean to hurt your feelings! I'm sure it's a very good poem, it's just that I've never been into poetry, I don't know much about it—"

I didn't wait to hear the rest. I closed the bedroom door and put the magazine down on the dresser and threw myself across the bed. Even the pleasure I'd felt at Dad's praise—at Dad saying he loved me, as he'd loved his own father—was spoiled.

Why couldn't she at least have pretended to like the poem?

Why had Consuela told her she was selfish and disagreeable? What had Mom done to *her*?

I swallowed hard, feeling really disappointed, and rolled over on my back to stare up at the ceiling. My eyes were stinging, but she wasn't going to make me cry.

"David, we're going to eat now," Mom called through the door.

I imagined her standing there, smiling, thinking everything was great because she was going to get that big check. I wanted to hit her.

"David?"

"I'm not hungry," I said loudly.

"Of course you're hungry. You're always hungry." She sounded calm and reasonable.

I gritted my teeth. "I'm not hungry! Leave me alone."

I wanted to yell at her, but Consuela said yelling usually just made things worse. How much worse could they get, though, if your own mother didn't care anything about you or try to understand you?

"What's wrong with David?" I heard Dad's voice in the background.

"I think he's sulking," Mom said, and I could tell she'd turned away from my door.

"What's he got to sulk about? He was okay a little while ago."

"Oh, I think it's because he brought me this odd little poem, and I didn't rave about it—he'll get over it. He can eat when he feels like it."

"What did you say about his poem? Gail, you didn't put it down, did you? *Say* you didn't like it?"

Mom sounded defensive. "Well, I could hardly pretend to understand it when I didn't, could I? Something about a treasure chest . . . David doesn't have a treasure chest that I know of, unless he's talking about that cigar box he keeps all that junk in, and how is that like *him*? He's the most peculiar child. . . . What am I supposed to do, pretend I think his poem is wonderful when it's just . . ."

They moved back out into the kitchen and I couldn't make out the words anymore. I didn't want to. I didn't want to know what they thought.

Why did they have a kid if they didn't want to make the effort to understand anything about me? I wondered.

I knew they were sitting out there eating deli salads and cold cuts with rye bread, and they were talking about me. Or, more likely, they'd already forgotten about me.

Peculiar, she'd said. The most peculiar child.

How was I peculiar? How could I be any different from what I was?

I rolled over on my stomach and buried my face in the pillow again, bumping the dresser with my elbow hard enough to make it hurt. That stupid old teddy bear fell off the top and landed on me, and I threw it off on the floor.

I lay there until it got dark and I was hungry, but I didn't go get anything to eat.

Why was I the way I was? Even Dad, though he'd said he was proud of me, that he loved me, didn't really seem to understand me. Not the way he would have if I'd been a jock instead of a clumsy klutz. Why couldn't I have been the kind of kid whose parents could understand him?

There was no answer.

4

There was nobody home when I got up the next morning. My parents had already gone to work. I was really starved from last night, and I'd been looking forward to a good solid breakfast, maybe pancakes or even waffles, if Mom had time to make them. Sometimes when she didn't have an appointment until late, she didn't go to work until midmorning.

No Mom, but there was a note under the saltshaker. "David," it said. "Don't make a mess. I'll be interviewing a new maid this afternoon, so pick up after yourself."

I looked at the clock. I didn't have time to make either pancakes or waffles and clean up too. I decided to fry a couple of eggs.

Only we were out of eggs. We were also out of milk and orange juice. Mom had forgotten to pick up the groceries that Consuela would ordinarily have bought. I settled for toast with peanut butter and a glass of water.

It wasn't a very good day. Tim had a cold and a sore throat, so he stayed home from school. I missed two words on the spelling test. I wadded up the paper and threw it away. If I took it home, Mom would want to know why I didn't get one hundred percent. She always said, "Couldn't you try a little harder, David, and get an A?"

So I didn't show her my papers very often. Only when there were no mistakes.

At lunchtime they ran out of chocolate milk just before I got there, and then Willy Curtis tripped Georgie Eisenberg as he was walking past me. Georgie lost control of his tray and dumped coleslaw, spaghetti, and red Jell-O on top of my head.

It was a mess. Everybody but Georgie laughed when it trickled down my back and my front and slid onto the floor. Mrs. Haines, who had lunchroom duty, told me to go home and get cleaned up, and she sent Willy to the office.

I felt embarrassed walking home looking as if someone had thrown up all over me. I decided I wouldn't go back to school that afternoon. Maybe by tomorrow the kids would have stopped laughing about it.

I didn't realize Mom was home until I walked into the living room and came face-to-face with a large lady in a flowered dress. She stared at me as if I'd just crawled out from under a rock.

Mom turned red. "For heaven's sake, David, what have you done now?"

Why did she just naturally assume I'd done something stupid? Anger stirred inside of me. "Georgie accidentally spilled his tray on me," I said, and my voice shook a little.

"Well, go get cleaned up," Mom said, then turned to the large lady. "When could you start, Mrs. Talmadge?"

The lady pursed her lips, still looking at me. "Well, I don't know. I'm not sure I want to work in a household with young boys in it."

I froze. This person, in place of Consuela?

"There is only *one* young boy," Mom assured her, "and David's very well behaved. He's neat and quiet. He won't give you any trouble."

Neat and quiet, I thought. I didn't want to be either one. I wanted to be like Tim, who was allowed to leave a few crumbs or a wrinkled bedspread without it being a federal case.

Mrs. Talmadge wasn't convinced, probably because I looked as if I needed to be hosed off. "I thought I was being asked to keep house for a *couple*," she said. "No, really, Mrs. Madison, I am not a *baby-sitter*. I don't think you'll suit me at all."

She rose to her feet and picked up her purse. "You'll excuse me. I have another interview at four o'clock."

When she had gone my mother turned on me. "Why on earth did you have to come home *now*, and looking as if you just crawled out of a garbage can? If she hadn't seen you, she'd probably have taken the job."

"But I'd still have been here later," I protested. "They sent me home from school. I couldn't go to class like this."

"Go get cleaned up. I'm going back to the office," Mom said crossly, and left me there alone.

Red Jell-O made a streak down the side of my face, and I decided I'd have to take a shower as well as change my clothes. As the water pelted down on me I clenched my fists. It wasn't fair. Mom was *never* fair.

When Dad walked in that night, Mom had just come in. She broke the news to him that she wouldn't be home for dinner. "I have an appointment with Dr. Kingsley and his wife to show the house on Grand Avenue. Wouldn't it be something if I made two major sales in just a few days?"

Dad scowled. "It would be something if you stayed home and cooked a meal," he said. "What are David and I supposed to eat?"

"There are leftovers in the refrigerator," Mom said breezily, and headed out to earn more money. What good did it do to earn more money when we never did anything fun with it? Tim's family went on picnics, went to Disneyland, played games, laughed and had fun, and I didn't think they even had much money.

One of the casseroles in the refrigerator had mold in it; Consuela hadn't had time to clean that out before she was fired. Dad made a sound of disgust and left the dish on the counter for Mom to handle later. He found some soggy salad, rejected that too, and finally settled on leftover roast, cooked carrots, and garlic toast. We had ice cream for dessert.

Dad looked at me across the table as we finished. "I guess the cleaning woman Mom was interviewing didn't work out?"

I swallowed. "No. She doesn't like kids. At least not boys."

Dad made a snorting sound, and I wondered if that meant he shared her opinion or not. "Well, stack the dishes in the dishwasher. I have to go out to a meeting. I'll be home by ten."

So I had this wonderfully exciting evening all by myself, watching reruns. I wondered if there was any way I could get myself adopted into Tim's family, but I figured probably not. Some of the other kids' mothers worked too, but most of them were home in the evening, not always having appointments to show houses.

Mom came home about nine, in a better mood than she'd been in during the afternoon. "Have a good evening?" she asked but didn't wait for me to answer. "Isn't it time you were in bed?"

"Yeah, I guess so. I was just having a snack."

Her smile faded. "And leaving the kitchen looking like a hurricane just struck. I don't understand why you always have to leave such a mess, David. Wipe up the counter. Put those wrappings in the trash. Why can't you remember those things?"

"I was going to clean up," I said quietly. "You just got here before I had time to do it."

"Well, do it now and get to bed." She dropped some brochures on the table alongside her purse and stepped out of her high heels, standing on one foot to rub the other one.

I wiped up the crumbs beside the brochures, then paused to look at them. There was a rustic-looking house set in some trees, and I spoke without thinking.

"Boy, that's a neat place. Why can't we get a house in the country, Mom? Then I could have a dog." I'd wanted a dog ever since I could remember. "Maybe with this big commission you have coming—"

She sighed loudly. "David, your father and I don't want a house in the country. We like an apartment, where someone else does all the maintenance, and we're handy to our jobs. And I've told you before, *no dogs*. They're dirty and messy, and they need more attention than we have time to give them."

"I'd take care of it," I said. "I'd keep it clean and feed it and everything."

She turned away, carrying her shoes. "I don't want to talk about dogs," she said.

Other people in apartments had dogs. They walked them in the park. They had them for company when they were alone at night. What I really wanted was a great big dog, like a German shepherd or a Great Dane or a golden Lab, but I'd settle for even a little dog. Dad liked dogs—he'd had dogs when he was a kid—but he wouldn't argue about it with Mom, he said.

I went into my bedroom and shut the door, but a minute later the door was opened and Mom stuck her head in. I flinched even before she spoke.

"Apparently it didn't occur to you to run a load of washing while you were doing nothing this evening. There's no maid to do the laundry, thanks to you. All you have to do is put the clothes in the machine, add the detergent, and turn it on."

"I . . . I didn't think about it," I said. "Nobody mentioned doing the laundry." It wasn't fair. I'd never done the laundry. Why should I suddenly be expected to do it?

"No. You don't think. Well, I've put in a load now, but you'd better run another load when you get home from school tomorrow. And be sure you leave your room looking good in the morning, so the next applicant for the maid's job won't think you're always a slob. Make your bed."

"I ran out of time this morning," I said defensively. "I had to clean up the kitchen, and I didn't want to be late to school."

"All right. Just *think*, David. You make seventy-five percent of the work around here, and you're old enough to take care of at least part of it yourself."

She turned and left without saying good night.

My throat ached. On the dresser old McGoo stared at me with his beady little eyes and I suddenly reached out and punched him in the face.

He tipped sideways, still smiling.

Ashamed, I set him up straight and muttered, "Sorry. It's not you I'm mad at."

I didn't even feel foolish, talking to a teddy bear dressed like a police officer. After all, who else was there to talk to?

It was better when Tim got over his cold and came back to school. "Hey, guess what?" he greeted me.

He was grinning, so it had to be good. "You're getting that van your dad was looking at," I guessed.

"No. He said that one had too many miles on it. He's still looking. No, it's better than a new van."

"What, then?"

"We're getting a dog."

"No kidding?" I was sorry it wasn't me getting it, but I was still glad for Tim. "What kind?"

"A black Lab. We're going over on Saturday to look at them. There are ten in the litter, and Mom says we can have one. They're almost eight weeks old, and we get first choice."

"Wow! That's great," I said, and meant it. Maybe I could sort of share it, since I was at Tim's house so much. Maybe it would like me too.

I mentioned it at dinner that night. For once, both my parents were home. Mom had made another sale and she was in good spirits. She even cooked steaks and baked potatoes instead of picking up something at the deli.

"The Pattons are getting a puppy," I said. "A black Lab."

"Good," Dad said. "Labs are nice family dogs."

"I interviewed another housekeeper today," Mom said. "Her name's Nell. She hasn't agreed to come yet, and I haven't told her that we have an eleven-year-old son."

Dad grinned and reached over to tousle my hair. "Don't tell her about David until you've got her hooked. Can't have her scared off by our resident monster."

He was kidding, but I couldn't help wondering. Was it really my fault that we couldn't get a maid? I was a kid, and I couldn't do anything about that.

My folks watched TV that evening, and I went in my room and wrote a story about a kid with parents who didn't appreciate him, so he made soup out of them and shared it with his six dogs, who were all gigantic slavering monsters. It was stupid, but it made me feel a little better.

5

O ver the next few days Mom interviewed two more women to take Consuela's place. One of them was fat and insolent, Mom said. I saw her when she was leaving and I was glad Mom hadn't hired her. Nobody with a mouth permanently turned down that way was going to talk to me the way Consuela had, or be a friend.

I didn't meet the other one, but Mom talked about her enough so I wasn't sure I'd have wanted her, either.

"She wants two dollars an hour more than I paid Consuela," Mom said while we were eating salad and spinach soufflé, which I hate.

Mom was frowning, but Dad tried to keep it light. "Well, you're the new millionaire in the family. Pay her! Then we'll all be nice to her, and maybe she'll stay."

Mom flashed him one of those looks. "We'd have to be nice to her, all right. You should have heard her list of demands! Won't work Tuesdays under any circumstances, won't carry out garbage—"

"David can carry out the garbage," Dad interrupted, but she didn't pay any attention to him.

"Won't shampoo carpets, won't clean up after pets—"

"We don't have any pets," I said wistfully, and she didn't pay any attention to me, either.

"She doesn't want to do any of the shopping—"

"The way Consuela did," Dad reminded her. "Consuela was a jewel, Gail. You shouldn't have offended her."

Mom made a face at him. "She was the one who offended me, remember? Don't keep interrupting, Jerrol, I'm trying to tell you how she gave me this long list of things she won't do. What's the use of hiring someone if they won't do the things you need to have done?"

"Well," Dad said mildly, helping himself to more salad, "*you* don't want to do them. That's why you're trying to hire someone else, right?"

Mom was exasperated. "The person doing the hiring should be able to specify what she wants done."

Dad nodded. "Sure. But the person doing the work has the right to decide what she'll do, I guess. If you didn't suit each other, keep on looking. Or call Consuela and apologize and ask her to come back. Tell her David talked you into it because he misses her." He grinned in my direction, and for a moment I felt a leap of hope.

Mom quickly squashed that idea, though. "I'm not

the one to do the apologizing in that situation," she said. "*She* was rude to *me*, incredibly rude. She said unforgivable things."

My hope died. I poked at the soufflé with the disgusting green stuff in it and wondered if I could get away with dumping it in the garbage when Mom left for her evening appointment. I could fill up on peanut butter and jelly sandwiches if she left in the next few minutes.

I tried changing the subject. "There's an open house at school on Friday. So you can see the progress we've made before the end of school. Last time this year."

Neither of them had come to anything at school after the open house last September. I had a couple of things on display I was proud of, and I wanted my parents to see them.

"Friday?" Mom echoed. "Oh, honey, I'm sorry, I can't on Friday. Barry's called a dinner sales meeting, so I won't even be home."

I looked at Dad, but he was shaking his head as he pushed back from the table. "No dessert tonight? Okay, guess I'm better off skipping that anyway, no more exercise than I'm getting. Sorry, chum," he said to me, "Friday's out for me too. I promised Bill I'd take his place in the bowling league finals that night. Can't let a friend down, you know."

He stood up, and I swallowed hard, looking after him as he left the kitchen. Couldn't let a friend down, but nobody seemed to mind letting me down every time I wanted something.

Mom was getting up too. "Clear the table, David, will you? I have to run. I'll make it up to you, about missing the open house. Okay?"

She gave me a distracted smile, bent to kiss my cheek, and spun around, already forgetting me. "This shouldn't take long. I'll be home early."

I wondered what they'd think if they came home and I wasn't there. If I just disappeared from the face of the earth. I wondered if they'd even notice.

When Mom called, "See you later," I didn't answer. As soon as she was gone I scraped the spinach soufflé into the garbage can and made myself a couple of sandwiches, but I wasn't really in a mood to eat them.

At Tim's house, nobody ever spent the evening alone. There was always someone around. They read books out loud, or watched TV together, or played board games around their big old dining room table. There was always lots of noise and clowning around.

When was the last time anybody in our family had whooped in laughter over a silly game?

The doorbell rang.

I got as far as the living room and stopped. I wasn't supposed to let anybody in when I was home by myself.

Close to the door, I said, "Who is it?"

"Open up, David! It's me," Tim's voice said.

He was grinning from ear to ear, and it was easy to figure out why. He was carrying a shiny black puppy, hugging it against his chest.

"You got the dog!" I said, stepping back so he could come in. "Wow! Can I hold him?"

Tim handed the pup over. "It's a her, not a him," he told me. "Her name's Daisy."

She was soft and warm and wiggly. Her tail was wagging a mile a minute, and an eager tongue reached out to lick my chin.

It sent a good feeling through me, and I stroked the satiny black fur. "Daisy. Are you going to be my friend, Daisy?"

Tim watched me, his hands in his pants pockets. "She's everybody's friend. Especially if you feed her."

"Does she like peanut butter and jelly? Let's go see!"

Tim followed me into the kitchen, where I tore off a little bit of one of the sandwiches. Daisy gobbled it down, and I gave her some more.

"Gosh, you're lucky," I told Tim. "I wish my folks would let me have a dog. She's sure cute."

"It's probably because you live in an apartment. If you had a house like ours, with a fenced yard, you could probably talk them into it. Dogs need a place to run."

Daisy had finished the sandwich and was licking my arm. "She's sure got big feet," I observed.

"Dad says Labs always have big feet. She'll grow into them and the rest of her will be big too."

I put her down, and she skidded on the vinyl floor, then took off, with us after her. She went exploring.

"She smells everything," Tim pointed out. "She chews on stuff too so watch her."

As he spoke, Daisy paused to nibble on the corner of a magazine that was sticking out from the bottom shelf of the coffee table.

Chewing wasn't all she did.

A minute later, in the middle of the living room carpet, Daisy suddenly squatted.

Tim yelped and dived for her, but he was too late.

She was piddling there between Dad's chair and the couch.

The timing couldn't have been worse, because right then I heard a key in the lock and Mom walked in.

"It's just me," she said. "I forgot my . . ."

And then she saw Tim and Daisy and the widening stain on the carpet.

Tim's eyes were wide with shock. "I'm sorry, Mrs. Madison," he said. "I'll clean it right up."

Mom went first pale and then bright pink. "Get him a rag, David," she said, sounding as if she'd just been strangled. She reached for her briefcase, sitting beside the door, and backed out of the room. "Get it all up with the rag, then sprinkle baking soda on that spot to get rid of the smell."

I got the impression that if she hadn't been civilized— or maybe just in a hurry—she'd have throttled all three of us, Tim and me and the dog.

"Jeez, Dave, I'm sorry," Tim muttered.

"Yeah," I told him hollowly as I went to find a rag.

Daisy frolicked along with us, nearly tripping me. And when we got down on our hands and knees to clean up the place she had wet, she licked our faces and wagged her tail.

I knew I hadn't heard the last of it. When she came home, Mom was going to tell me exactly what she thought of dogs, and Daisy in particular.

"I don't know how I survived being a baby," I said. "I mean, babies are messy, and they're a lot of work. Mom never liked messes, and I think babies are more work than puppies."

"My mom doesn't like messes, either," Tim said. "But she just makes us clean them up."

I nodded. I wasn't even allowed to make any.

Just before he left, I blurted out the question that had been on my mind for weeks, off and on. "Tim, do your folks ever fight? I don't mean hit each other, nothing like that, but argue?"

Tim looked uneasy. "Not much," he finally said. "Once in a while they disagree about something, and sometimes they go in their bedroom and talk, but they don't yell or anything."

"Mine do," I said soberly.

Tim wet his lips, picking up Daisy and holding her so she could reach his neck and chin to kiss them with that warm pink tongue. "Do you think . . . they're going to get a divorce, David? Like Billy's folks?"

We knew this kid at school, Billy Kringen, whose folks got a divorce, and he wanted to live with his dad, but the judge said he had to stay with his mother until he was fourteen. Then he could choose. He missed his dad a lot and only saw him every other weekend.

"I don't know," I said, and felt my eyes stinging. "I just wish they didn't argue so much."

Tim sounded as subdued as I felt. "I'll see you," he murmured, and once more I was alone for the evening in our apartment.

I woke up in darkness except for the dim glow from a streetlight through my bedroom curtains. In the distance I heard a siren—an ambulance, maybe, or a police car—and I thought that was what had interrupted my dream about living in this wild house in the country with twenty dogs and a swimming pool.

Then I heard voices from my parents' bedroom across the hall. They were arguing.

I couldn't make out the words, only the fact that they were angry.

I pulled the blanket over my head, but it didn't shut out the voices. After a minute in which the words got louder, I threw off the covers and sat up. I didn't want to know what they were saying, but if I had to be kept awake, I might as well know why. I got out of bed.

As soon as I opened my door, the words became clearer.

"You are so selfish, Jerrol, I can't believe it!" Mom said, sounding as if she were talking through her teeth. "You travel all over, regularly, and when I barely mention going on a trip you come unglued!"

"I travel on business, part of my job," Dad shot back.

"It's part of my job too! This conference could be a valuable one!"

"You're talking about a month of lounging around a pool in Hawaii, after the conference, with a bunch of people I don't even know, and leaving David and me here alone!"

"I said you could come too, for heaven's sake!"

"You know darn well I can't take a month off to do something like that! I've got a job of my own, remember? There are bills to be paid!"

"I told you how big that commission is going to be! I'll pay more than my share of the bills, pay for the trip. It's the first time I've ever had a chance to do anything like this, and I want to go, Jerrol! It's an opportunity to meet a lot of important people, people who can help me in my career!"

"In Hawaii?" Dad sounded almost too controlled. It meant he was furious.

I glanced across the darkened room at my clock's big red digital numbers. Twelve-ten, when they'd usually be fast asleep.

I hated the way they sounded. Not like people who loved each other and were part of the same family, but as if they disliked each other. The way they sometimes sounded when they talked to me if I'd done something wrong—or even suggested an idea they didn't agree with.

"Well, why not Hawaii if there's a better opportunity there?" Mom demanded. "I want to go, Jerrol."

"Alone? Because I can't go with you."

"Won't go, you mean. You could take the time off if you wanted to. You have a vacation coming."

"I have two weeks coming, and I've already arranged to spend that fishing with Jim Kapp along the Stilly. I can't let him down."

"But you don't mind letting me down," Mom said.

Dad finally let loose a bunch of swear words. "You just thought this up, Gail! I've already made plans and now you expect me to let my best friend down on a camping trip we've been planning for six months! Wait until next year, and I'll try to get the time for a month wherever you want to go."

My feet were getting cold, but I stood there listening, unable to go back to bed. I wanted to yell at them to stop, but I couldn't make a sound.

"I don't want to wait until next year," Mom said, in that tone that means she's being reasonable when everybody else is irrational. "This is a special trip, special rates, special people. It won't come together again next year. I'm going to go, Jerrol."

"I can't go," Dad said.

I curled my right toes over my left ones, trying to warm them up. My fingers were digging into the door frame until they ached.

"Then I'll go by myself," Mom said.

Up to now the only comfort I'd had was that they didn't seem to be fighting about me. And then Dad said it.

"And what are we going to do about David while you're gone for a month?"

I stopped breathing. A painful lump plugged up my throat, and the ache began to work down into my chest.

"We can find someone to look after David," Mom said after a moment's hesitation.

"Who?" Dad asked softly. "You never even gave any thought to David, did you? I can't keep him by myself, Gail. Your trip starts the seventeenth, right? On the twenty-third I have to fly to Chicago for a week of seminars and sales meetings. And on the fifth of next month I'm hosting all the bigwigs from New York for three days. All day and every evening."

Again there was a small silence. I hurt all over now. She *hadn't* thought of me at all when she was making her plans.

"If you hadn't fired Consuela," Dad said now in a cruel way, "*she'd* probably keep him. Or do you plan to leave him with one of your housekeepers who don't like kids?"

I imagined her swallowing as she tried to think up an answer. "I'll ask Mama if she'll keep him."

Dad snorted, but it wasn't from amusement. "Oh, I can just see Grandma Elsie entertaining him in that mauve silk apartment with the white carpets nobody's allowed to walk on with their shoes on. What's he supposed to do there? Too far from home to play with his friends, with a lady who thinks she's a movie star and takes a nap every afternoon with cucumber slices over her eyes? So David sits on one of those thousand-dollar antique chairs and pretends he's a statue for thirty days? Eating caviar and drinking Elsie's favorite champagne?"

No, I thought, almost saying it out loud. Not there. I hardly dared to breathe when I went to Grandma Elsie's. Everything she had was expensive and breakable.

"We'll ask her to come here," Mom said uncertainly.

"And sleep where? Your mother on the couch in the living room? Or put David out there, and let her have his room, sharing it with Officer McGoo? She'd have to have a board under the mattress, and there isn't room for all the luggage she'd have to have to stay anywhere for that long. Her makeup kits alone would fill David's entire room."

"So now you're going to start in on Mama again."

"I like your mother all right," Dad said, in a tone that suggested he was not quite telling the truth. "But she never raised a boy, she got rid of her husband years ago, and she knows nothing about men or boys. That apartment of hers is a show place. She's got things of her own to do, anyway. Isn't she scheduled to go on a cruise next month with those fancy new friends of hers?"

"Oh. I'd forgotten."

I waited, shivering.

"Well," she said after a moment, "we'll have to figure out something to do with David. But I'm going to Hawaii, Jerrol. It's the chance of a lifetime."

"Maybe Ma would take him."

"*Your* mother? Oh, Jerrol, you know what she's like!

She's not fit to take care of a child, she'd let him run loose—"

"She raised me," Dad said. "And I don't think I turned out so bad."

If Mom answered, I didn't hear her. I didn't hear anything more, and then the crack of light under their door disappeared.

At last I went back to bed.

"What are we going to do about David?" Dad had asked, and it scared me.

I buried my face in the pillow and wondered how they'd feel if they found me there, suffocated, in the morning.

At least it would solve their problem of what to do with me.

6

I could hardly bear to look at my parents the next morning. Surely, after the things they had said late last night, they would be different.

Only they weren't. Mom had an apron tied over her dress and was cooking frozen waffles in the toaster. Dad was buried, as usual, in the morning paper. Sometimes he read something aloud to us.

Neither of them looked directly at me. I slid into my chair, feeling sort of queasy and more tired than I usually did in the morning. I hadn't gone to sleep for a long time after I eavesdropped on their conversation.

How could they talk about what they were going to do with me while they went on about their own business and then act perfectly normal when we were all together?

What was normal? I suddenly wondered. Normal at Tim's house was nothing like this. Of course they had two boys instead of one, and Mrs. Patton didn't go away to work at the hospital until ten o'clock, so she wasn't in a rush to get out of the house herself. They'd all be talking at once, rounding up shoes and lunch boxes and books, and they'd have the radio on, so even if nobody was talking it wouldn't be silent like our house.

Except when they were disagreeing about something, my folks didn't talk that much. They weren't paying any attention to me, and I sneaked a look at Dad's face. I didn't think he was aware that Mom and I were there at all.

All at once I felt as if I'd gone away from them. I was invisible, they wouldn't notice if I was there or not, and I was viewing them from the wrong end of the telescope, so they looked distant and small and not real.

"Anybody want another waffle?" Mom asked, and Dad closed the paper.

"No, I'd better run. See you tonight."

I didn't answer; I hadn't touched the two waffles she'd already put on my plate. Mom had even poured syrup over them, as if I were a little kid who couldn't be trusted to pour out half the pitcherful. It would be sickeningly sweet, and if I tasted it I would throw up, I thought. And Mom would believe I was sick and let me stay home today.

But she didn't even notice I wasn't eating. She had had a plate beside the toaster, taking an occasional bite, just standing at the counter. She took the last forkful, rinsed off the plate under the faucet, and put the plate in the dishwasher.

"I have to run. I have an early appointment at the beauty parlor," she said, still not looking at me. I listened to her high heels clatter across the floor, then felt swallowed up in the quiet as she left me alone.

The telephone rang.

I looked at it, not wanting to answer it, but it kept on ringing. Finally I went over and picked it up.

"Hello?"

"Oh, David, dear. Good morning." It was Grandma Elsie. She didn't want to be called Grandma. I think she felt she looked too young to be a grandmother.

"Good morning," I said now. "Mom and Dad have gone to work."

"Oh, my. I'd hoped to speak to your mother. I suppose I'll have to try to catch her at the office. How are you, dear?"

I tried to say I was fine, but my throat closed on the lie. She didn't notice. She hadn't waited for an answer. "Well, I have to leave in a few minutes, so I'll call the office."

I finally managed to speak. "She's at the beauty parlor."

She thanked me cheerfully and hung up. I was feeling strange again, as if the adults in my family were sort of on the other side of a sheet of glass. They spoke to me, but they didn't really see me or hear me.

Did any of them really care if I ever answered?

For a minute I thought about not going to school, and then I decided it wouldn't be worth the trouble it would cause. So I went, but I might as well have stayed home for all I learned that day.

Mrs. Crandall had to speak to me twice when I lost my place during social studies, and I'd left my math homework on the desk at home, so I got marked down for that, and during PE Mark Tate hit me with a pitched ball and I dropped in the dirt thinking my shoulder was broken.

Except that it hurt pretty bad, I hoped it *was* broken. Maybe if I had to go into the hospital somebody would pay attention to me in some way besides bawling me out.

Only the nurse said it was just bruised and I could go back to class. It was a stinking day.

Tim walked home with me, his face sober. "You okay?" he asked, and I grunted.

"Great," I said. "Except for hurting."

He knew I meant more than hurting in the place where a purple bruise was spreading over my shoulder. "What do you think your folks will do with you if your Mom goes to Hawaii?"

"I don't know. They haven't mentioned the subject to me. It's like it's none of my business what they do, not even what they do with *me*."

"Let's play with Daisy, okay?" Tim said, and I was glad to change the subject.

Mom's car was out front, so I knew she was home when I finally got there. I'd deliberately stayed at Tim's as long as I dared.

Dad showed up about the time I reached our door. He gave me a tired smile. "Hi, son. Let's hope your mom's not annoyed with us for being on the late side. I've had a rough day and I'm not exactly in the mood to cope with an angry lady."

"Me neither," I said with feeling, but it didn't do us much good.

I hadn't had any breakfast, and lunch had been creamed chicken and peas on toast—ugh!—so I headed for the kitchen to have a snack.

Mom was there, looking around at us coolly from the sink where she was peeling vegetables. "Well, it's about time, David. Since you left such a mess this morning—again—I thought maybe you'd come home early enough to clean it up before I got here."

My mind was a blank. "What mess?"

"You never took a single thing off the table. Left your breakfast on the plate, the butter and syrup still sitting there. I'm busy, David. I don't want to come home as tired as I always am and have to clean up the mess you left in the morning."

I couldn't think of anything to say, at least not that I dared to say out loud. She didn't even wonder why I hadn't eaten anything.

"Don't apologize or anything," she said grimly. "Honestly, we don't expect much of you, David. Once in a while it would be nice if you made an effort to help a little when you know how rushed we always are."

What about all the times I *had* cleared the table and loaded the dishwasher? I wondered. Didn't that count for anything? Didn't it make any difference that I'd been too upset to eat, worrying about the plans my parents were making that they weren't telling me about, plans to dump me on someone who probably wasn't going to want me?

Grandma Elsie always acted glad to see me and kissed me dryly on the cheek. She bought me nice presents at Christmas and on my birthday. But she never talked to me, not more than a few words, and then she didn't give me a chance to answer. I knew Dad was right that she wouldn't want me to stay in her apartment. It wasn't the kind of place any kid would want to go, either.

Grandma Ruthie, Dad's mother, probably wouldn't want me, either. I only saw her on holidays, when she came to Everett or we met her in Seattle and we all went to a restaurant. On Thanksgiving last year, when everybody else had turkey and cranberries, she had a big taco salad and a plate of refried beans and rice. Mom rolled her eyes at her own mother behind Grandma Ruthie's back.

I didn't know her even as well as I knew Grandma Elsie, because she lived a lot farther away. The presents she usually gave me were neat and different, though. An Ant Farm, once, which was fun to watch until Mom decided most of the ants were dead and she threw it out. Another time the present had been a book and some rubber stamps with Egyptian hieroglyphs so you could use them for code to send secret letters. Tim and I used them to communicate during class for a while until we got caught.

I remembered lots of things Mom had said about Grandma Ruthie. I knew they didn't care much for each other. "I'm common as an old shoe," Grandma Ruthie had said, and later Mom asked Dad what was so great about being common, for heaven's sake?

There wasn't anyone else, though, for me to stay with for a month while Mom was in Hawaii. No relatives, anyway. Most of Mom and Dad's friends didn't have kids, they had careers. They traveled, they went out to dinners, they had nice houses or apartments like ours, and some of them had boats on Puget Sound. Their homes weren't likely places to leave an eleven-year-old boy.

I wished they'd bring up the subject, maybe ask my opinion—though I didn't have one except I didn't want to stay with anybody—but they didn't.

"No luck getting someone to clean yet, I guess," Dad said.

Mom turned on a stove burner under a pan. "No. Nobody wants to work for anyone who has kids, nobody wants to do all the things I want to have done. They've all gotten so independent it's unbelievable. Before you've even begun an interview, they'll say they won't do this or that, or they have to have one thing or another."

"Well, it's too bad we can't get Consuela back," Dad said, and Mom gave him a hard look before he turned and went on through to the bedroom to get rid of his jacket and tie.

I went into my own room and dropped my books on the bed. I wished they'd just *talk* to me, I thought desperately.

And then when they finally did, I wished they hadn't.

7

Mom and Dad were so normal during dinner that they kind of calmed my suspicions. I mean, they only sniped at each other a little bit, and they made a few jokes and laughed about them. I began to hope maybe the stuff I heard them talking about in the night had all blown over. Maybe they'd talked it out and decided that Mom wouldn't go away, after all, and so they wouldn't need to do anything about me.

Only I looked up from my last bite of apple pie to catch the look that passed between them when Mom stood up to clear the table, and I knew that it hadn't been settled yet. At least not the way I wanted it to be.

Dad cleared his throat, and Mom avoided looking directly at me.

"David, we need to talk to you about something," Dad said.

I put down my fork, the pie still on it, as my stomach tightened up like it was suddenly filled with rocks.

I waited.

"It's almost time for school to be out," Mom said. "And we're trying to make plans for the summer."

Dad cleared his throat again, and I made my hands into fists under the table and didn't say anything.

"You know your mother has a big commission coming soon," Dad said. "She's decided to take a trip with part of it. Some others from her office are going to Hawaii for a convention, then staying on for a month, and she's joining them."

"I haven't been able to find a housekeeper who can stay with you," Mom said. "Grandma Elsie might have, but she's already made other plans—"

"I can stay alone," I managed. "I won't get into any trouble. And Mrs. Patton doesn't care if I spend a lot of time over there with Tim."

"We don't think that would work very well, son," Dad said. "I made a few phone calls, tried to get you into a summer camp, but all the ones that take kids for more than two weeks are already filled. So we've made arrangements to take you out to Grandma Ruthie's while Mom's gone. I talked to her today, and she said she'd be glad to have you."

I slid a glance at Mom. Last night she'd said, "Oh, Jerrol, you know what she's like. She's not fit to take care of a child—" Yet here she was now, listening to Dad, and she wasn't saying a word about how unfit Grandma Ruthie was.

"I'll drive you out there the Saturday after school ends," Dad said, and then he looked relieved and pushed back his chair, and Mom looked relieved and whisked around cleaning up the kitchen, and I sat there looking at that last bite of pie.

Neither of them asked me what I thought about their scheme. Neither of them waited around for me to say anything. It was all settled. I was going to Grandma Ruthie's for a month.

I didn't even know Grandma Ruthie, not really. I saw her on holidays, and she gave me neat presents, but I didn't *know* her. She lived a long way off, out on the coast, and I'd never even been there. Dad sent her money for bus tickets when he wanted her to come and see us—which wasn't very often—and she usually went back on the bus the same day, after we'd had dinner together.

It would be like going to live with a stranger.

I was afraid and angry, and I didn't know what to do about either one.

Tim's family was planning all kinds of things to do during vacation. They were going on camping trips in the Cascades and to the ocean beach. They'd go hiking up to the Ice Caves near Verlot, and drive down to Portland for the Rose Festival Parade. Even when they stayed home, they'd have fun.

I got more and more quiet, thinking about *my* summer. Nobody noticed except Tim.

"Did you tell them you don't want to go to your grandma's?" he asked.

"No. It wouldn't do any good. They've made up their minds," I said.

"How do you know? Maybe if you cried and kicked your feet and banged your head on the floor, and screamed that you didn't want to go—"

He was trying to be funny, but I didn't feel funny. What I felt like, actually, was crying and kicking my feet and banging my head on the floor, but I knew it wouldn't work. Mom was determined to go away for a month, and Dad had his plans all made too, including what would happen to me.

Mom helped me pack my suitcase the night before we were to leave. Mom folded up shirts and shorts and jeans and put them in the open case. She chattered away about how much I was going to enjoy being at Grandma Ruthie's, and I wondered if it was so much fun why they'd never bothered to take me there before, even for a short visit.

"You don't even like her," I said, watching as she put in a stack of underwear.

A pink spot appeared in each cheek. "That's not true, David," she protested, adding some socks.

"You said she wasn't fit to raise a child," I added, and then remembered too late that I wasn't supposed to have overheard that. "I mean, I heard you say once that she hadn't done a very good job of raising Dad."

"When did I say that?" she asked, pausing to look at me. But I guess she thought she must have said it, because it was truly the way she felt. "That was just a joke between your father and me. Because he has to be reminded to pick up after himself. Ruthie never made him do that when he was your age."

"But you don't like her," I persisted. "You told Dad she was a silly old woman when she refused to stay in a hotel last year instead of taking a long bus ride home late at night."

"I only meant I wouldn't have turned down an offer of a motel room. She could easily have gone home the next day." I didn't say anything, and she gave me one of those looks. "I'm sorry we didn't have an extra bed so she could stay with us, but we offered to pay for the motel bill. There, I think that's everything unless there's something you want to add."

The school magazine was lying on the dresser. I reached up for it and dropped it on top of my clothes in the suitcase. And then, without even meaning to, I grabbed Officer McGoo too and crammed him into a corner.

"Oh, David, you aren't going to take a *teddy bear* with you? You aren't a baby anymore." Her expression said that if I took McGoo, I *was* a baby.

"He's just something familiar," I muttered. "Something I'm used to." I slapped down the lid and started trying to shut the case.

She didn't say anything else about the bear, but I could tell she was ashamed of me. I guess I was sort of ashamed too, but I didn't back down.

Dad and I left around eight the next morning. We didn't even have breakfast before we started out.

"We'd just disturb your mom if we putter around in the kitchen," Dad said. "We'll let her sleep in and we'll get something on the road."

It was a long way to the town of Little Beach. We had sausage-and-egg sandwiches at a McDonald's and then stopped again for burgers before we got there, around one o'clock.

"This must be an awful bus ride," I said. "No wonder she's always tired when she gets to Everett to visit us."

Dad gave me a quick look, as if I'd criticized him for making her travel so far to share holidays with us, but he didn't say anything.

The sign said LITTLE BEACH—POPULATION 312.

"This is it?" I asked incredulously as we slowed down for the little town.

The highway was the main street through Little Beach. In fact it was almost the only one except for a couple of little short cross streets that had maybe two or three houses on each one.

There was a general store, a tiny post office, a gas

station, and a peculiar little building with amateurish signs stuck all over its barrellike exterior that said BURGERS, POP, ICE CREAM, SOUVENIRS, POSTCARDS. The barrel was painted an unappetizing shade of blue.

That was all there was, except for the cluster of small houses with most of their paint scoured off and the tiniest white church I ever saw.

An old man sat on the porch in front of the general store in one of several rocking chairs. There was a big orange cat on the railing in front of him. Down the street, a little kid was riding a Big Wheel. There were no other people.

"Ma likes it here," Dad said. "I told her it would be easier for us to take care of her when she's old if she'd move to Everett or Seattle, but she hates cities."

I hadn't wanted to come, and I'd been dreading our arrival, but I never expected this dreary little place.

What was I supposed to do here for a month, the best part of my summer vacation?

No movies, no mall, no skating rink, no library. No anything.

I tried to control my voice. "Looks like a fun place."

"You'll enjoy the beach, I think," Dad said, and I could tell from his voice that he was feeling guilty about bringing me here.

I didn't see any beach. Dad gestured with one hand

as we turned onto one of the side streets. "The ocean's just beyond the dunes, here. It's less than a five minute walk from Ma's. Great beach. You can't really swim here, of course. Because of the undertow."

What was I supposed to do with the ocean if I couldn't swim in it? I wondered bleakly.

Dad took us jouncing over the unpaved street, and we stopped in front of one of the little houses. This one was pale yellow. There was no lawn and no trees, just a sandy front yard with some tufts of tough-looking grass here and there.

It didn't look as if anybody lived there.

And then one of the curtains twitched aside for a few seconds, before it fell back into place. A minute later Grandma Ruthie appeared at the doorway.

Usually when I saw my grandmothers they were dressed up for eating out. Grandma Ruthie wasn't dressed up now; she didn't look anything like the grandmother I knew.

She was wearing shapeless and almost colorless pants and a baggy dark red sweatshirt that said DON'T ASK ME, I DON'T KNOW on the front of it, and running shoes.

She came out to meet us, smiling. "Hi, David. Hello, Jerrol."

"Hi, Ma," Dad said, getting out and opening up the trunk to get out my suitcase. "How's it going in Little Beach?"

"Exciting as ever," she said. "We're gearing up

for the church rummage sale, and this season's souvenirs just came in at the Burger Barrel. Thrilling as it ever gets."

I wasn't sure if she was kidding or if that was really all the excitement that ever happened here. I suspected, with a sinking feeling, that she *wasn't* kidding. Grandma Elsie never kidded about anything, but once in a while Grandma Ruthie had made some dryly humorous remarks. Nobody ever laughed, but I *thought* they were intended to be funny.

"Come on inside," she said now. "I've just baked a blueberry pie. Picked the berries last summer and had them in the freezer, waiting for an occasion. Having my son and grandson come has to be an occasion, right?"

She was smiling, but somehow I had the feeling she was needling Dad. I couldn't remember when he'd ever come all the way out to the coast to visit her. I sneaked a look at him, but if the needle got to him, he wasn't showing it.

Dad forged ahead with the suitcase, and Grandma came along with me. I wanted to fall back and not go into the house. Somehow that would make it final, that I was stuck here for a month, if I went inside. But there didn't seem to be anything else to do.

It was not only a small house, it was old. I looked around quickly as we went through the living room. It sure wasn't anything like the place where Grandma Elsie lived.

There was no carpet, only faded floral linoleum, and Mom would have sent every piece of the furniture to a dump, I thought. Not that it was junk, exactly, but it was worn and scratched. There was a couch, covered in faded flowered material that didn't match the flowers on the floor. There weren't any easy chairs, only a rocking chair with a red cushion in it, facing the tiny television that stood on a low table.

"Through here," Grandma Ruthie was saying. "Sorry I didn't have enough warning to get my stuff out of the back bedroom, David. But I guess it won't hurt you to sleep in the room with the sewing machine and a stack of boxes. They'll fit in the attic—the boxes, I mean—but it's so hard to get them up there I don't bother."

It was about half the size of my room at home, and there was no carpet in here, either. The linoleum was made to look like boards with pegs in them. There was a bed with a chipped white metal headboard, a dresser, and a straight chair, plus the sewing machine she'd mentioned and some cartons piled along one wall.

The calendar on the wall, the only decoration in the room, was from 1973.

"If you want to stay overnight before you head back home," Grandma Ruthie said to Dad, "you can share the bed with your son."

"No, I better get on back today. I'll stay long enough

for that pie, though." Dad dumped the suitcase on the bed and seemed not to notice the kind of surroundings he was leaving me in.

We went back toward the living room—I got a glimpse through open doors into another bedroom and a bathroom—to the kitchen. It was nothing like home. My heart sank with every step I took. How come I had to be *here* so my mom could go to a luxury hotel in Hawaii?

The kitchen was almost as big as the living room, and it looked like something out of an old-fashioned movie, one made back maybe in the 1940s, in black and white. Linoleum again, red and white checked curtains and tablecloth on the big round table. A funny old-time stove that had the oven sticking up on top on one end, beside the gas burners.

No dishwasher. No microwave.

But I could smell the pie. We sat down at the table and she dished up the pie, with a scoop of ice cream over each piece, where it quickly began to melt. I swallowed the queasiness I felt and tried it.

"You can still cook, Ma," Dad said. "I always said you made the best pies in the county."

Grandma Ruthie nodded. "Nobody but me makes pie crust from scratch anymore. It's easier to buy it already rolled out, from the store. And I make it with a sugar substitute these days. You want a glass of milk with yours, David?"

It was good pie. I began to have hope that at least I wouldn't starve to death here. Of course I might die of boredom, from the look of this place.

As soon as Dad scraped the last of the purple juice off his plate, he stood up. "Well, guess I'd better get rolling." He reached out and gave me a hug, one arm around my shoulders. "You be good, David. I'll call you. And thanks, Ma, for taking him."

"No problem," Grandma Ruthie said.

I walked out to the car with Dad, while she stayed behind. I thought maybe he'd hug me again, but he didn't, just patted me on the back.

"Take care, son. Have a good time," he said.

I stood there watching while he turned the car around, and we both waved. Then he was gone.

I drew in a shaky breath. A month here, a whole month, I thought. With an old woman I hardly knew, in a place that didn't look as if it would provide much in the way of entertainment. There wasn't even a library, and I'd only brought a couple of books with me.

I'd write my own stories, then, I decided, swallowing the lump in my throat.

I turned around and walked back to the house, determined not to think about the ache in my chest. Trying not to think that my mom, just so she could go off on a trip to have fun, had been willing to leave me here with a grandmother she had said wasn't fit to raise a child. She hadn't even gotten up to say good-bye.

I opened the front door and went inside, trying to pretend that everything was okay, when I felt as if I were an eggshell, cracking all over. Breaking apart. Dying.

8

"**W**hy don't you call me Ruthie? Everybody else does," she said when I went back into the house.

I nodded, not trusting my voice to speak yet. Dad hadn't looked around and waved again before he turned the corner onto the highway, though I'd watched him as long as I could.

"I have to run over to the church for a few minutes. You want to come along and meet Pastor Grady?" she asked.

I shook my head and made myself speak. "No. We got up real early and I'm tired. Maybe I'll . . . take a nap."

It was a baby thing to say. Mom would have told me that, or said I was avoiding reality. Maybe I was. I didn't like reality when it meant being away from my friends, when my folks didn't care enough about me even to ask how I felt about anything.

Ruthie smiled. "Okay. I'll see you later, then. Explore, if you don't feel like sleeping. Sometimes it's hard to get used to sleeping in a new place."

It sure was. After she'd gone I walked through the house, seeing more things this time. There were a lot of bookcases in the living room, and magazines and papers on the tables and on the floor beside the rocking chair. Mom would never have left our place looking so cluttered, but it would have felt sort of homey if I hadn't been so lonesome already.

There was a black iron stove I hadn't noticed earlier. A wood stove, judging by the rough wooden box beside it where a few sticks of kindling stuck out the top. I didn't know anything about wood fires, except that I'd seen open fires in the fireplace at Tim's. Mom didn't care for fires; she said electrical heat was so much cleaner. I looked around, but there didn't seem to be any other kind of heat here.

I went down the short hallway, pausing to look into Ruthie's room. It was nicer than the one where I'd be sleeping. It had more bookcases, and a bright colored quilt on the bed, and some pictures on the top of the dresser.

I was surprised at the pictures. There was one of Dad that had to be his high school graduation photograph. He looked young and happy, grinning out at me. There was Mom and Dad's wedding picture too. He looked older, but just as happy, and Mom was smiling too, with her veil thrown back and holding a bouquet in front of a white dress with a lot of lace on it.

And then there was me. More pictures than I even remembered having taken. One for each year I'd been in school, including one where I was missing two teeth. And then a bunch of snapshots, mostly when I was younger.

There was one that I lingered over, because I didn't remember seeing it before. Maybe when I was about three years old. We were on a beach, Mom and Dad and I, in bathing suits. Everybody was laughing and I had mugged for the camera, so I looked silly. Silly, but happy.

When had we stopped doing things like going to the beach or on picnics or hiking together? When Mom went to work selling real estate, I thought, and she had to be dressed up all the time and didn't want the wind to blow her hair or anything to break her fingernails or get her clothes dirty. Or had it been even before that? I couldn't remember. I thought maybe it was Dad who liked to do things outdoors, that maybe Mom never really had.

I turned away from the picture of the family that no longer existed.

Across the hall I looked into the bathroom. The tub was so old it was up on curled feet; it had been enameled lavender like the lid on the toilet. No shower. There was no linen cupboard, just open shelves with towels and other stuff on them.

I went on to "my" bedroom.

It was strange, unwelcoming.

The suitcase was still in the middle of the bed. I swung it over onto the top of the sewing machine. I probably ought to unpack it, but I didn't feel like it. Taking my clothes out of it would be making sure I had to stay here. For a little while I could pretend that wasn't so, that Dad was coming back and taking me home.

The boxes of Ruthie's stuff made it seem more like a storeroom than a bedroom, and that was all I wanted it to be. I wasn't going to *live* there, just stay a few days. I wouldn't even let myself think about it being a whole month.

The bed felt harder than my bed at home, and the plain white spread had an unfamiliar texture. The pillows were practically flat, and I put one on top of the other. When I lay on my back, I could see a stain on the ceiling where it had leaked once.

I had promised myself I wouldn't cry, but the tears kind of leaked out a little. I felt them trickling into my ears.

But I really was tired, and I guess I fell asleep.

I woke up suddenly, and even before I opened my eyes or remembered where I was, I felt somebody looking at me.

I rolled my head toward the door, expecting Ruthie, but she wasn't there. A slight noise, sort of a whimper, brought my gaze downward, and closer.

I jumped when I saw the dog. At least I guessed it was a dog. I'd never seen one quite like it.

It was big, tall enough to be resting its square muzzle on the edge of the bed beside me. It had thick wiry hair, black and brown, and friendly brown eyes. When I looked at it, it whimpered again, and at its back end a stubby tail began to wag.

"Who're you?" I asked, sitting up.

Ruthie spoke from the doorway. "This is Susie. She keeps me from getting lonesome. Susie, this is David."

Susie's tail wagged harder as I put a hand out toward her.

"Does she bite?" I asked cautiously as the dog licked at my hand.

"She's definitely a lover, not a fighter," Ruthie assured me. "She'll probably want to sleep with you."

I gave her a startled look. I couldn't imagine Mom letting a dog get on a bed, but apparently Ruthie wasn't kidding.

"Can she do tricks?"

"Not that I know of," Ruthie said. "She doesn't even bark to be let out. She comes and puts her head in your lap and looks at you and wags her tail."

"What is she?" I asked. By this time I dared to touch her head, and it wasn't at all soft, like Tim's pup, but had stiff, springy hair.

"She's an Airedale. She loves to go on the beach. She'll keep you company anytime you go there. You slept for a couple of hours. Are you hungry yet? The stew's done."

I was, I realized, starving. I got off the bed, and Susie followed me, licking at my dangling hand as we headed for the kitchen. Stew sounded better than spinach soufflé.

It was delicious. Ruthie had baked biscuits on top of

it, and I stuffed myself before we even got to more of the blueberry pie. So far so good, as far as food went, I thought.

After we'd eaten, Ruthie asked, "Do you want to wash or dry?" She started running water in the sink.

I shrugged. "I never did either one."

"Nothing to it. I'll wash, you dry. You might as well learn which cupboard each thing belongs in. Use that towel there. I don't suppose Gail messes up her fingernails by getting them in dishwater."

"We have a dishwasher," I told her. I felt peculiar, sort of halfway standing up for Mom even though I was pretty angry at her.

Ruthie nodded. "Expensive dudes, though I guess for someone working away from home they're real handy. I used to think one day I'd be able to afford one, but living all by myself, it's really an unnecessary expense."

The idea popped into my mind that Dad could afford to buy her a dishwasher. Or a microwave, or a new stove.

Doing the dishes wasn't bad, though. It only took a few minutes.

"It'll still be light for a couple of hours," Ruthie said. "Why don't you take Susie for a run on the beach?"

"Where is it? How do I get there?"

"It's right over the ridge. Just keeping going to the end of the road, then follow the path. Susie knows the way. Give her a good run."

"Okay," I said. It might help to have a dog, though I'd rather have had a puppy.

Susie ran eagerly ahead of me. There were two more houses past Ruthie's place on our side of the road, one on the other side, before the road petered out in the sand. I slogged up over the dune, and before I saw the ocean I heard it.

The wind was blowing hard, lifting Susie's ears as she paused to look back at me. Then she was gone, down the other side, and a moment later I too reached the top.

Susie was racing ahead of me across the widest stretch of beach I could have imagined, sloping ever so slightly toward the surf that must have been a quarter of a mile away, rolling toward me in slow motion. I could hear it, louder now that there wasn't a dune between it and me.

They called this place Little Beach, but it wasn't little. It stretched in both directions for a long way, and there was nobody on it except Susie and me and, far to the south, a lone figure out in the edge of the surf.

Can't swim here, Dad had said, because of the undertow.

What was there to do on a beach if you couldn't swim?

And then I realized the boy down the beach was flying a kite.

Susie was going in the other direction, but when I yelled at her, she swerved back and galloped toward the boy. He was too far away for me to see clearly, so I couldn't tell how old he was, but I felt a flicker of hope. Was there a kid here who might be willing to be friends?

I'd met Tim in kindergarten, and we'd been best

friends ever since. Sometimes we did things with other kids, but mostly we just ran together because we liked the same things and we understood each other. I'd never had to make friends anywhere else, and the idea made me nervous, but the thought of spending half the summer here with nobody to talk to except Ruthie was discouraging.

I kept walking toward the kite-flier. After a while I could make out the kite better; it was bright colored and it had a long tail and a dragon's head. I'd never flown a kite, and I was impressed by how he made it dip and turn and glide in long, graceful swoops.

Susie had found a dead sea gull and was bringing it to me. "Ugh! It stinks," I told her, but she trotted proudly along with the smelly thing in her mouth.

There were all kinds of things on the beach besides dead birds. Live gulls overhead and little birds running along in the edge of the surf, besides all kinds of shells and remains of jellyfish and crabs and sand dollars. I still had a perfect sand dollar I'd found on the beach when I was just a little kid.

I spotted one now and bent to pick it up. This one was perfect too, unbroken, and I slid it into the pocket of my jeans.

By this time I was closer to the boy with the kite, and I began to try to figure out what to say to him, in case he looked in my direction. Something brilliant would be best, I thought. Like "Hi. You live around here?"

He wore jeans, rolled up a couple of inches, and a

blue windbreaker, and his back was toward me, his attention all on the dragon kite high above him.

Susie had finally dropped the dead sea gull and rushed up to him, leaping up on him so that he looked down at her.

"Hi, Susie," he said. "Get down."

So he did live nearby; he knew the dog's name.

I opened my mouth to speak when he turned to see if Susie was alone, then found the greeting wiped out of my mind when I saw his face.

It was hardly like a face at all; for a moment I thought of a Halloween mask, one of those soft plastic ones that's molded into a grotesque shape intended to scare little kids.

He stared at me, and I stared at him, and my mouth dried up so I couldn't speak.

Suddenly, with his attention distracted from it, the kite plummeted toward the beach. He jerked around, manipulating the line he held, but the kite plowed into the edge of the waves. He ran toward it, lifting it out of the water as tenderly as if it were alive.

I stood rooted in the sand, but he didn't turn around. My heart was pounding. I'd never seen a face like his except in a horror movie. He was doing something with the kite, and I realized he wasn't going to turn back toward me.

It made me feel strange, as if I'd intruded on someone's privacy, even though he was on a public beach.

Scar tissue, I thought. It had to be scar tissue. What had happened to him?

I felt shaky, as if I'd just witnessed some terrible accident.

Mom and Dad always taught me not to stare at people who were different—deformed, dressed funny, things like that. It would make them more self-conscious than they undoubtedly already were.

But this boy was so unexpected I hadn't been able to keep myself from staring, and I hadn't been able to think of a thing to say. I guess the best thing would have been to just say hi, the way I'd intended, but it was too late for that now. He'd seen the shock in my face, at the way he looked.

I walked back the way I'd come, not even noticing the grayish sand or the noisy surf. Susie ran ahead, circled around, chasing gulls, barking senselessly at the little sandpipers or whatever they were. When I called her back, she came practically flying, with her tongue hanging out and her ears swept back, and leaped right against my chest, knocking me flat.

I glared at her. "You stupid dog. What did you do that for?"

Susie enthusiastically licked my face, ignoring my efforts to hold her off, until I managed to get to my feet.

She kept leaping around, but at least she couldn't reach my face anymore. I looked around for the path we'd used to come to the beach, but all I saw was a long line of dunes with scrubby grass and brush growing on it.

I turned and looked toward the boy with the kite, who was a long way off down the shore. Had I walked past my own path?

There was no way to tell. I was making footprints on the wet sand, but where it was dry I hadn't left a trail.

"Which way to go home?" I asked Susie.

She grinned at me with her tongue lolling.

"Go home," I said to her. "Take me home."

She took off, but not toward the dunes or any path. She headed for the water where a flock of gulls had landed, scattering them.

"All right, you dimwit. I'll find the way without you," I told her.

But it made me feel uneasy, knowing I was sort of lost, and the sun was sinking out there beyond the ocean.

9

I plowed through loose sand to the top of the ridge. There were houses down there, all right, but none of them was Ruthie's. I couldn't see hers, in either direction.

Susie came bounding up beside me, panting, and I tried again.

"Which way to go home?"

She sat down, waiting for me to decide. "Jeez, what an idiot you are," I told her. She wagged her stubby tail as if I'd praised her.

Nervously, I glanced back over my shoulder. The tide was way out, leaving what looked like a mile of sand between me and the water. I didn't see the boy with the kite and the scarred face. The sun had dropped to the horizon, leaving a scarlet streak between the clouds and the water. In a short time it would disappear. It was getting cold.

It was silly to be scared, I told myself. These houses in front of me had to be in Little Beach; I hadn't walked *that* far. And even if Susie didn't understand what I was saying about leading me home, she'd probably go there eventually, when she got tired.

It was just that this was so different from Everett, where there were streets and house numbers and telephones to call from, and people. I was used to people. There were lights in the nearest of the little houses, but no people.

"Well, let's walk along the top of the dune—that way," I decided aloud. "Maybe I'll recognize the right path when I come to it."

There were actually paths all over the place, none of them leading where I wanted to go. I saw an old man on one of the streets, but when I called out he didn't seem to hear me.

And then, when I was beginning to think I must have walked on past the right path—or maybe turned in the wrong direction in the first place—I recognized the figure in the dark red sweatshirt that looked almost black in the twilight. She climbed the dune and stood there waiting for me.

"Nice out here, isn't it," Ruthie said when I was close enough.

"Uh . . . yeah," I said.

"I love to walk on the beach. It's the main reason I'd never consider going to live in town, far away from it. It's quiet, and peaceful. You get ulcers living in town, or have nervous fits and need to see a psychiatrist. You don't need any therapy here except the sound of the surf. It's so soothing, and it puts things into perspective. Here I am, this one little person with my insignificant problems, and there's the mighty Pacific—stretching out there for seven thousand miles, all the way to Australia and even Antarctica—and it's the same as it's been since the earth was born. And my problems sort of melt away."

Ruthie was smiling, and I wondered what problems she had, and didn't really understand how the ocean could solve them when it didn't actually do anything but move in and out.

"Susie take you for a good walk?" she asked cheerfully, scratching the Airedale's head.

"I guess." I felt suddenly very homesick. I wondered if Dad was home yet, and how they felt there in the apartment without me. Did they miss me, or were they just glad they'd solved the problem of what to do with me?

"I saw a boy on the beach, with a kite," I said, so I wouldn't think about home.

"Probably C. J.," Ruthie said. "One of the Bedrosian kids. That's their house at the end of our road, on the other side. The one with blue shutters."

"There are some other kids in Little Beach, then," I commented as we started down the other side of the dune.

"Not too many, but a few. Mostly we're old folks here, bought our houses before the price of beach property went sky-high. The way they keep raising taxes, though,

I don't know how long we'll all be able to afford to stay here."

I looked at her face, a dim oval in the fading light. "What will you do if the taxes get so high you can't pay them?" I knew a little bit about that kind of stuff because my mom talked about it. I knew some people lost their homes when they couldn't pay the taxes.

"Sell, I guess," Ruthie said. "My house isn't worth much, but the property is. The developers would be in here in a minute if we'd all agree to sell."

I knew about developers too. Mom was always delighted when one of them built a whole slew of new houses for her to sell. She liked developers. I got the idea that Ruthie didn't.

"So far, though," Ruthie went on, "nobody is listening to their offers. We're not talking about property, we're talking about our homes. There, that's where the Bedrosians live. Six kids."

Six. What would it be like to have five brothers and sisters?

I spoke without thinking. "I wonder if Mom would have stayed home instead of having a career if there were six in our family instead of only one."

"I don't think Gail's the stay-at-home type," Ruthie said. "She enjoys having a career. Me, I never aspired to a career. I just worked when I had to, when things were tough with Grandpa Frank, when he got hurt, or when he was between jobs. I was a waitress, which is hard work and doesn't earn anywhere near as much as I guess your mother earns."

And besides, I thought, my mom didn't really like kids all that much. Not like Tim's mom. *She* liked what she did away from home too, at the hospital. Like talking to old people, or sick ones, and reading to them, writing letters for them, that kind of stuff. She talked a lot about patients she met there. But she always enjoyed her family too. So it wasn't just having a job that made the difference. I couldn't really imagine Mom having six kids. She didn't even care much about the one she did have.

I didn't want to think about that, so I looked at the house across the road from Ruthie's. The Bedrosian house was a little bigger than hers, not much. The lights were on inside, and I could see people moving around, warm and safe. I caught a glimpse of a girl's face, laughing, and then she was gone.

The homesickness swept over me again. Sometimes my folks made me mad, and they weren't around very much of the time, and didn't pay much attention to me when they were, but I missed them.

"Are there any other kids my age besides the Bedrosians?" I asked.

We'd reached our front yard. "Not many," Ruthie said. "You'll meet them, either on the beach or at church."

I swallowed. "We never go to church."

"Your dad did when he was your age. Church and

Sunday school, every week." She opened the door and walked inside; I noticed she had left it unlocked. We never left our door unlocked. "You'll like Pastor Grady," she assured me, leaving me with a sinking feeling. Everything was so different from at home, and I couldn't believe how lonesome I was already.

Susie almost knocked me down going through the doorway. Ruthie looked back and laughed when I slammed into the doorframe.

"She forgets that only one person can be in a certain space at one time," she said. "Or maybe nobody ever taught her that."

Ruthie had a fire in the black stove; it had windows in the front so I could see the flames, and the heat felt good. "I thought maybe we'd have some cocoa," she said, leading the way toward the kitchen.

I followed her and watched Susie squeeze her off to the side in that doorway, then push past her to rush to her dish. She didn't eat, though, but looked back at us.

"Go ahead, eat. We're going to stay here for a few minutes," Ruthie told her. "She doesn't like eating alone," she explained to me. "She usually waits until she has company before she'll dig into her dish."

I slid into a chair at the table. "She's kind of a . . . funny dog," I suggested.

"Oh, she's different, all right. I don't know who had her to begin with. She wandered in here wet and cold and hungry and with an injured hip after she'd been hit by a car out on the highway, I think. Nobody ever claimed her, so I just kept her. Whoever had her before didn't teach her much, and I haven't had time to do it, either."

Susie had come over to nose at my leg, and I said, "Sit, Susie."

She wagged her tail.

"Sit! Stay!"

She licked my hand.

"She's kind of dumb," I dared to comment.

"Oh, I don't think she's dumb. She just hasn't been taught. Might be a job for you. You like marshmallows in your cocoa?"

She tried to make it a good evening for me. We watched a movie on TV until way past my usual bedtime, and had cookies and cocoa, and neither of us said very much. When she got up to turn off the TV—it was a small one, with no remote, but at least it was color—she stretched.

"We'll go to church at about quarter to eleven, unless you want to go to Sunday school first."

"No, thanks," I said quickly. "Good night, then."

"Good night, David." For a minute I was afraid she was going to hug me. Instead, she said, "See you in the morning."

I decided I wasn't dirty enough to need a bath in that big lavender tub, so I just brushed my teeth. It felt peculiar getting into an unfamiliar bed, and stranger yet to lie there in total darkness.

There were no streetlights, no sounds of traffic. Only the distant rush of the surf, muffled by the dune that stood between us.

The homesickness had slid away a little bit for a while, but now it was back. How was I going to stand it for a whole month?

I buried my face in the pillow, which wasn't anything like my own pillow at home, and didn't know whether I loved my parents, because I missed them, or hated them for leaving me here.

In the silence I heard the faint sounds of Susie's toenails on the linoleum floor. A moment later a wet nose nudged my cheek.

For a few seconds I hated her too, because she didn't belong to home, and she didn't seem to be very bright, but then I reached out my hand and touched her wiry fur. For a long time she stood there, resting her muzzle on the edge of the bed, licking whatever part of my hand or arm she could reach, while I kept my hand on her. I wished she were soft and comforting, like Tim's pup Daisy, but she was better than nothing.

CHAPTER 1

For a moment, when I woke up, I couldn't think where I was. There was the smell of frying bacon and coffee, and then Ruthie's voice. "Go wake him up, Susie."

A few seconds later I heard her toenails again and remembered where I was.

Susie approached and once more rested her muzzle on the edge of the bed. When I rolled my head toward her, she wagged her tail.

It all came back to me then. I was at Ruthie's, and today my mom was flying to Hawaii, and my dad was probably reading the Sunday paper and planning on doing some fun thing later with one of his friends.

I wouldn't exactly say my day turned out to be fun.

To begin with, it was so foggy I could hardly see across the street. But by the time we'd had breakfast and done the dishes, the sun was burning through. "Take

Susie for a run, why don't you, while I pack a basket for Smiley. Then you can carry it for me, and we'll be back in time for church."

"Who's Smiley?" I asked. Susie had heard the word *run* and was dancing all over the kitchen, stepping on my feet, leaping up in the air. "Down, Susie. Sit." But she kept on wagging her tail and bouncing off the walls in anticipation.

"Smiley's our neighbor on the next street over. He's an old bachelor, and he has diabetic retinopathy, so he doesn't get out much. I take something over for him to eat a couple of times a week." Ruthie had a basket lined with a dish towel, and in went the last of the blueberry pie and something in a covered dish.

Trying not to regret the disappearance of the pie, I asked, "What's diabetic retinopathy?" It didn't sound very good.

"Mean's he's going blind because of diabetes. He can't see well enough to do much cooking. Go on, get that fool dog out of here."

Outside, Susie didn't seem quite so foolish, because she just ran, making a beeline for the beach. This time, with the fog all over everything, I knew I had to pick a marker so I could find my way home, and then I realized that a pair of big logs had washed up high against the dune. I made sure what they looked like, then went on after Susie.

There was no one else on the beach, which wasn't as wide as it had been yesterday. The tide was in. The fog made it cool too, so I didn't linger too long. A beach, I decided, was only fun when you had a friend there to do things with.

I thought about the boy with the scarred face, C. J. Bedrosian. It wasn't likely he'd ever want to be friends after the way I'd gone into mute shock just seeing him. I went back to the house fairly soon.

Old Smiley turned out to be a gentle old man who couldn't see us very well but urged us to take seats. He acknowledged Ruthie's introduction of me with a smile and seemed delighted with the food in the basket.

Then we went to church. It was such a tiny place it could only hold about fifty people, but it was full.

I'd been to church with Grandma Elsie a few times, but this was different. Everybody sang as if they enjoyed it, and Pastor Grady turned out to be a man about Dad's age who talked about how to get over being depressed. If you wallowed in depression, he said, it was because you were only thinking about yourself. Think about other people, he told us. Don't be selfish. Think how lucky you are compared to someone who's hungry, or has no place to live, or is blind or crippled or suffering from loneliness or disease.

I squirmed because I *had* been feeling sorry for myself. I had reasons, though, didn't I? My parents were the ones who were selfish. They were doing what *they* wanted, not what was good for me.

Just ahead of us sat the Bedrosian family. Ruthie had spoken to the parents when we sat down, and introduced me to the closest ones. Not to the older kids, though. They sat off to my right, and the boy didn't look at me. The girl, about my age, smiled. She was the one I'd seen through the window last night. "I'm Catherine," she murmured, and feeling self-conscious I said, "I'm David."

I was pretty sure the boy next to her was C. J., but he didn't turn around so I could see his face, at least not then.

I didn't know whether to be glad or sorry that we hadn't been introduced.

During part of the sermon, I looked around the congregation. There was another boy about twelve or so, and one maybe a year younger. They kept whispering and laughing behind their hands. Maybe they'd be worth meeting. While I was watching, the lady next to them reached over and poked the nearest one, putting a finger on her lips.

Ahead of me, the one I thought was C. J. shifted position and rested his arm along the back of the pew, carefully not touching his sister. After a minute or two, he cautiously lifted his finger and lightly brushed the far side of Catherine's neck.

She twitched and put her hand up there, while the boy moved out of the way. A minute or two later, he repeated his performance, tickling the back of her neck.

She rubbed at it impatiently. The next time, he took hold of the zipper on the back of her dress and began to ease it down, very slowly. He had it open about four inches before she realized what was going on.

She swatted at his hand, but I saw that she was laughing silently. It was C. J., all right. He was laughing too.

It made me feel peculiar in a way I couldn't describe, to see that face laughing. Somehow it didn't seem that anyone so badly scarred would find anything funny about life.

Just before we sang the last hymn, Pastor Grady said, "Don't forget, our hot dog roast on the beach will be at six. Everybody's welcome to come early and help build the fire, especially our visitors." Was he looking at *me*? My face burned. "Oh, and Ruthie, this time we'd appreciate it if you locked Susie up at home. Last time she got away with a big package of wieners."

Everybody laughed, including Ruthie.

On the way out of the church, Pastor Grady shook hands with me and said he hoped I was going to have a good summer at Little Beach. Then he asked, "Have you met some of the other boys? Harold, Lyle, come and meet a summer visitor, David Madison."

Harold was the bigger, better-looking boy, the one who'd been shushed. Lyle was the smaller, quieter one.

"Hi," Harold said. "Lucky you, to be spending your vacation in this great metropolis where there is absolutely nothing whatever to do and nobody but Lyle to do it with."

I wasn't sure what to say to that, so I tried to smile at Lyle.

"It's better than having nobody but Harold to do anything with," Lyle offered. "You play ball?"

"Uh . . . not real well," I had to admit, not wanting to cut myself off from all contact with the only kids here except for the Bedrosians.

Ruthie was still talking to some old lady. Harold said, "You like Nintendo?"

"Sure." That was one thing we could share.

"I don't suppose you brought any new games with you?" Lyle asked. He was skinny and had a pale face and kind of spiky blond hair.

"No, I didn't even think of it. Maybe I can get my dad to send me some, though."

"You got any money?" Harold was bigger than I was, a little on the chubby side. "They rent videos and Nintendo at the store."

"Do they? Yeah, Dad gave me some money."

"Come on over after lunch," Harold suggested, "and we'll let you rent us a new one."

"Sure," I said again, though I was sort of taken aback at his immediate invitation to let me pay. "Where do you live?"

He jerked a thumb over his shoulder. "Down there. The big white house. Lyle lives closer to you. I'll get him and then we'll stop by for you, okay?"

It sounded better than walking Susie all by myself, or sitting home with Ruthie for whatever she did on Sunday afternoons.

The Bedrosian family had just come out of the church. When I saw them from the front, they all looked pretty much alike except for their sizes. Dark haired, brown eyed, slim. Catherine was the prettiest, prettier even than her mother. C. J. was so close to the same size she was that I couldn't figure out which was older.

C. J. looked at me, and then away. He walked within a few yards of Harold and Lyle, and I thought they weren't going to speak, although they must know each other. In a place the size of this one, there was no way they could have helped meeting.

And then Harold said, "Going to the weenie roast tonight, monkey face?"

For a second I didn't believe what I'd heard.

It was true, I guessed. C. J. did sort of resemble a monkey, because of some terrible accident I couldn't even guess at. I felt bad because I'd been stricken dumb when I saw him, but Harold was deliberately tormenting him.

C. J.'s eyes had swiveled toward Harold, but then swung away, and he kept on going without responding.

Harold and Lyle laughed, but I didn't. My heart was pounding.

The scars weren't fresh. How long had C. J. been having to take this kind of thing?

"Oh, there you are, David," Ruthie said. "Let's get home before my roast dries out so much we have to give it to Susie."

I was quiet all the way home, and so was Ruthie. She was used to being alone. I wondered if it was hard for her to have me there, to lose her privacy, to have to cook extra. I wondered if she hated having me as much as I hated being there.

Dad was right about her being a good cook. She made lots of food too. Grandma Elsie hardly cooked at all; she went out to restaurants. And the few times we had eaten at her place she'd served such small portions that Dad suggested stopping for hamburgers on the way home. I don't think anybody was ever hungry when they left Ruthie's table.

Lyle knocked on the door about one-thirty. "Hi," he said. "Harold's over at the store picking out the Nintendo. He told me to come get you."

I felt strange, going with him. He wasn't the one who had called C. J. "monkey face," but he'd laughed. I tried to think of something to say to him.

"You live here all the time?" was the best I could come up with.

"Yeah," Lyle said. "Since my ma died, Dad and I've been living here with my grandpa. On the street behind Harold's, in the place with the green shutters."

"I didn't see a school," I said, kicking gravel as we walked out toward the main road.

"We take a bus," Lyle said. "Where you live, Dave?"

"Everett." He looked blank, so I added, "North of Seattle."

"Oh, yeah. Harold used to live in Bellevue, and he hates it here. Nothing to do. He lives with his mom and his aunt Millie. They got the biggest house in town, but they don't have much money to go with it."

"I guess nobody has all the money they need," I said.

What was his mother like, that she didn't teach him to be nicer to people who were unfortunate, like C. J.? I didn't ask that, though.

It was a short walk to the general store. On a Sunday afternoon there were only a few people there, buying bread or milk or pop and choosing videos.

Harold was waiting for us. He had three Nintendos in his hand. "Here," he said, thrusting them at me to pay for.

I went to look at the titles, feeling that maybe since I was paying for them I should help choose, but Harold was impatient.

"Come on, I don't have any of these. Let's go."

Tim and I always had a lot of fun with Nintendo, but that afternoon was kind of a bummer.

We couldn't all three play at one time, so somebody had to just watch, and most of the time the watcher was me. Harold was the one who decided who got to play, and he hogged everything.

He lived in a nice house, and his mother seemed like a nice lady, but I couldn't imagine my mom letting me be as rude as he was. When she brought us some apples, Harold looked at them with a sneer and said, "Who wants fruit? Aren't there any cookies?"

She fluttered apologetically and said there weren't, and Harold said, "Well, bring us some pop, anyway."

No please, no thank you. I sometimes forgot, but it was kind of ugly to see somebody that probably never thought of those words in the first place.

It was getting late when I stood up and said, "I guess I better be going home."

"Wait'll Lyle and I have one more game," Harold said, in a tone suggesting that whatever happened, it was all up to him.

"No, I think I better go now," I said. My heart had begun to pound again. Harold might not be the best person in the world to cross, the way everybody I'd seen so far gave in to him. "I'll take the Nintendos back."

"Hey, heck, no!" Harold said. "They're rented for twenty-four hours. Until tomorrow afternoon."

I didn't quite feel like jerking the connections loose, so I nodded. "Okay. I'll see you later."

Lyle echoed, "See you later, Dave," without looking around. Harold didn't bother to speak at all as I left.

I walked home slowly, kicking at gravel, past the little kid who didn't seem to do anything but ride his Big Wheel. "Hi," he said to me, and I answered "Hi."

I felt as if I'd been away from Mom and Dad for months instead of only a day. Maybe, I thought hopefully, Mom wouldn't like Hawaii after all. Maybe she'd come home sooner. Like next week.

If you were depressed, the minister had said, it was because you were thinking too much about yourself. But what else was there to think about?

Ruthie was on the phone when I got there. "Oh, here he is now, Gail. Just walked in." She handed it to me, and I spoke eagerly into it.

"Mom?"

"Hi, honey. How's it going? You making any friends yet?"

I thought about Harold and Lyle. "Well, not exactly. Where are you?"

"At Sea-Tac. My plane's due in about ten minutes, so I thought I'd call you. I'm going to miss you, David."

"You don't *have* to go," I said.

"Oh, honey, yes I do. I'll call you from Hawaii if I can. It may be tricky to figure out the time zones. And of course I'll be really busy most of the time."

"Yeah. Is Dad with you?"

"No. I took the Airporter down." There was a moment of silence, and then she added, "We aren't exactly speaking at the moment. That's a poor way to part company for a month, but sometimes he's so unreasonable."

A sudden terrible thought hit me. "You *are* coming back, aren't you?"

She hesitated just a few seconds too long before she said, "Yes, of course I am."

I didn't even hear what she said after that. All I could think of was what if she *didn't* come back? What if she and Dad got a divorce because they were fighting all the time, the way Tim had said?

It was the kind of thing that happened to other kids I knew. One boy in our class had had it happen three times: His mother got divorced from first his dad and then two stepfathers.

"David? They're calling my flight, I have to run. Be good, honey," Mom said, and I didn't even have time to say good-bye.

What if she didn't come back, though? I thought, feeling panic. What if I had to choose which parent I wanted to live with? What if I didn't have any choice but just had to do whatever they decided?

There was a pain in my chest as I hung up the phone, and it didn't go away for a long time.

11

There were quite a few people on the beach ahead of us. More than had been in church: old people, little kids. Most of the ones in between were gathering driftwood for the fire they'd started, and some men were rolling big logs in around it to provide seats and cut off the wind. Pastor Grady was there in jeans and a sweatshirt. He gave me a friendly smile and remembered my name.

Except for me, everybody seemed to know everybody else. I felt awkward and out of place. Ruthie introduced me to some of the older people. The Senior Citizens, she called them. The ones who had lived here a long time, and were worried about rising taxes driving them out of their homes.

I didn't think my parents ever had to worry about something like that.

Thinking about them made me uneasy again. When

they argued, they usually got over being mad before very long. I didn't know if they would, though, if they were apart and each one of them was too stubborn to call and apologize.

The Bedrosian family was there, and I sat on the end of a log and watched them and wished I belonged to a family like theirs. There were four boys and two girls: Catherine and a little one about two. The younger ones were running around like sand fleas, swooping down on shells or feathers or whatever the tide had left behind.

Mr. Bedrosian was cutting sticks for roasting the hot dogs. Mrs. Bedrosian set to work putting things out on one of the logs, as if it were a table. Catsup, mustard, relish, onions sliced in a bowl, potato and corn chips. The little boys snitched pickles or chips when they thought nobody was looking.

Ruthie saw me watching and grinned. "This is going to be a really nutritious meal."

I was getting hungry, but from the look of things it would be a while before we started roasting weenies. I looked around to see if any of the few kids were doing anything interesting.

Two of the middle Bedrosians were tossing a ball back and forth. Not much going on.

But I was the only kid sitting down, so I got up and decided to take a walk. At least I wouldn't be so conspicuous that way, because there were other people strolling, way down the beach.

C. J. was one of them. I recognized his windbreaker. He didn't have his kite this time, and he was walking away from me, hands in his pockets, right on the edge of the surf.

I sort of wanted to catch up to him, to apologize for the way I'd reacted to seeing his face the first time, but I didn't quite dare. He'd have every reason to dislike me, though maybe not as much as he must dislike Harold and Lyle. So far they hadn't showed up, and I wondered if they were waiting for the work to be done before they appeared.

Up ahead of me, C. J. stopped, stood staring out across the ocean, then turned and began to come back.

Immediately, instinctively, I turned too so I wouldn't meet him. Then I cursed myself, my cowardice, but it was too late. I couldn't stay in this place for a month without meeting him when we lived just across the street from each other. Why not face him and get on with it? Maybe he wouldn't hold it against me too much, the way I'd looked at him. After all, he must be used to it if he'd been scarred for very long.

Somebody threw something on the fire, and sparks rose up like fireworks. I heard laughter, and my throat tightened. They were all having fun, and I wasn't really part of it, and my mom was out there somewhere over the Pacific, winging her way toward Hawaii.

For a moment it didn't register when a small figure in a pink jacket detached itself from the crowd around the fire. The littlest Bedrosian, running the way little kids do, as if they'll pitch on their faces any minute. She was heading straight for the ocean.

I expected someone to take off after her, but nobody seemed to notice she was gone. I quickened my steps, and the little girl ran on, almost to where the waves reached their highest point before they fell back.

You couldn't swim here because of the undertow, Dad had said.

I yelled then, I don't know what, but nobody heard me. The surf was too loud, drowning out everything but the cries of a few gulls directly over my head.

"Stop!" I called, but the little girl kept on, right into the water.

She hesitated a moment—not because she heard me, but because the water was cold, probably—and then she took a few more steps and fell down.

The next wave was a big one, and it washed right over her.

I screamed, then, but still nobody heard me, and I broke into a run.

When the wave receded, it dragged the little girl with it, though not all the way. For a matter of seconds she just sat there, her mouth open as if she were stunned. The next wave hit her full in the face and knocked her tumbling, and this time it dragged her farther out to sea.

I gave it all I had. Behind me I thought I heard C. J. yelling too, but by this time I was saving my breath. I pelted along the hard-packed wet sand, sure she was going to go all the way out and under before I could reach her.

I pitched forward onto my knees just as the next wave hit. The water filled my mouth and nose, but I grabbed for the little pink jacket and felt it come loose in my hand.

Desperate now, I grabbed again, and this time I got her arm. The rush of the water was so strong that I was afraid we were both going to be caught in the undertow; it was all around me, icy, up to my chest, and I couldn't get to my feet.

And then, as the powerful tug caught me once more, and I struggled to lift the little girl free of it, I felt a hand on the neck of my shirt, felt C. J.'s resistance added to my own against the sucking water. The sea withdrew, leaving me free of its grip for a few moments, and I scrabbled to my feet, dragging the little girl.

C. J. helped haul me up the beach, out of reach of the next of those deadly waves. I handed over his little sister, who had begun to cry, and stayed there on my hands and knees for a minute or so, spitting up salt water.

"You okay?" C. J. asked, and I nodded, still choking.

The people up around the fire had finally realized something was happening and came swarming toward us. Now that I was wet, the breeze felt icy, and I was shaking.

I couldn't stop even when I finally got to my feet. Mrs. Bedrosian had come running to get her baby, and Catherine was there with tears on her cheeks.

"I thought she was right there beside me," she whispered, and her dad gave her a hug of reassurance now that everything was all right.

The little girl, dripping down her mother's front, stopped crying and said, "I went in the water."

"Better get up by the fire," someone said, and we all moved in that direction. When I reached Ruthie, she gave me a look of concern. The Bedrosians all were thanking me, and Ruthie patted my shoulder.

"You better trot back to the house and change your clothes," she said.

The wind that had felt chilly now felt like ice, and my teeth had begun to chatter.

"I brought a change of clothes for Laurel," Mrs. Bedrosian said, "because she always spills something on herself. You'd better go home and change too, C. J. And bring another jacket for Laurel."

So we started home at the same time, together, not saying anything. We met Harold and Lyle coming to the picnic.

"Hey, you guys, don't you know enough to get into bathing suits before you dive in?" Harold asked, and they both snickered.

It wasn't funny, and I was cold and shaking. Neither one of us answered. When they'd gone on by, C. J. muttered under his breath. "Jerks."

"Yeah," I agreed. I knew how close I'd come to not grabbing hold of little Laurel in time, how close I'd come to getting drawn into that undertow myself.

"I'm sorry about the other day," C. J. said then, unexpectedly, not looking at me.

I stumbled in the sand, regained my balance, and wasn't sure I'd understood him.

"For what?" I asked, confused.

"When I turned around, and you saw my face. It's always a shock to people, but I don't exactly know how to warn anybody."

He was apologizing to me! I'd been feeling guilty but I didn't quite know how to apologize. Instead, I finally looked at him and asked, "What happened to you?"

"I went through a windshield," C. J. said matter-of-factly.

I sucked in a breath. "Wow," I said. "How long ago did it happen?"

He glanced at me, then concentrated on slogging through the loose sand. "A year and a half ago. I was with my cousin Al in his new car, and he was driving too fast. We went off the road and rolled. I wasn't wearing a seat belt."

I thought about Dad's insistence that I always buckle up.

"Al wasn't belted, either. He got thrown clear and fractured his skull and smashed up his shoulder. I went through the windshield. We were in the same hospital room for almost three months."

It made me feel even colder, thinking about lying there all that time, hurting.

"Does it still hurt?" I blurted, and then thought maybe I shouldn't have asked.

"No." We came up on top of the dune, then started down the other side. "Not anymore, not until they do another plastic surgery. I don't know yet when they'll do that. I've had two already."

"Tough," I said. I didn't know how much of the shakiness I felt had to do with having come close to drowning—or watching a little girl drown—and how much from hearing about C. J. and feeling rotten about the way I hadn't even spoken to him once I saw his face.

"First time I looked in a mirror," C. J. said, "I wanted to throw up. So I know how looking at me makes people feel."

Again I felt a compulsion to tell him I was sorry, but once more I couldn't quite come up with the words to do it.

"Is that all the name you've got?" I asked. "Initials?"

He gave me a challenging look, then said, "My whole name is Cecil Jordan. I hit anybody who calls me that."

I raised my hands. "Not me! My middle name's Ambrose, after my mom's dad, but I don't tell that to anybody, either."

We'd reached his house.

"I'll see you later," I said, and he nodded and lifted a hand as I went on toward Ruthie's place.

I went inside and had to fight Susie down, she was so tickled to see me. "Sit!" I kept telling her, but she didn't know "sit" from "roll over."

She followed me into the bathroom while I rubbed down with a towel until my skin was red, and then into the bedroom while I got a complete set of clean clothes. I didn't have another set of athletic shoes, so I put on heavy socks and hoped the wet would come through so gradually I wouldn't notice it much.

I forgot about Susie. When I opened the door to leave, she squeezed past me and took off running for the ocean.

I yelled at her to come back, but she just kept going. I hoped somebody noticed her before she landed in the middle of the hot dogs.

"Stupid dog," I said. C. J. came out to meet me as Susie disappeared over the ridge.

It made me feel peculiar when he grinned. He *did* kind of look like a monkey, with his face all twisted out of shape the way it was.

"I don't know if she's stupid," C. J. said, "or if she just never got trained. Like good old Harold," he added. When he saw my expression as we fell into step together, he said, "Ma says Harold would be all right if anybody taught him anything. His ma's afraid of him, and so's his aunt—he has temper tantrums, like a baby—so they let him run the place. So he's a spoiled brat. I don't know. I just think he's a jerk."

"He invited me over to play Nintendo and made me pay for renting the games," I said.

C. J. laughed. "Sounds like Harold, all right."

"Then he and Lyle played most of the games," I

added. Somehow it wasn't bothering me as much now that I was talking to C. J.

"Lyle wouldn't be so bad if he got away from Harold. He used to like me, before . . . this happened. But he's afraid to be seen with someone who looks like me, now."

I felt funny being with C. J. too, I thought. Only I was ashamed of it. How would I feel if I'd had a terrible accident that left me looking the way C. J. did?

I wanted to talk to him, but no more about this, not right now. "That was a neat kite you had out on the beach," I said, changing the subject.

"Yeah. The dragon one. I made it. You want to fly kites tomorrow?"

I felt a flicker of interest. "Sure," I agreed. Nobody would see us together on the deserted beach. And then I was more ashamed than ever. Maybe I wasn't any better than Lyle.

"Good."

We went over the top of the dune, toward the fire. There were figures moving around the flames. From here their voices were drowned out by the sounds of the surf. As we approached, though, we could hear shrieks from some little kids chasing each other and then one of them started to cry when Susie came out of the shadows and knocked him down.

She was Ruthie's dog, not mine, but I felt embarrassed. I was the one who'd let her get loose. "I always thought it would be fun to have a dog, but she's too rough. She knocks everybody over."

"Train her," C. J. suggested, and then we were there, picking up the little kid, shooing off that idiot of an Airedale.

"I see she got past you," Ruthie said, shaking her head. "I forgot to warn you, she's an escape artist."

"You want me to take her back?" I asked, though I didn't really want to make another walk to the house.

"No. We'll just keep an eye on her. We're about ready to start roasting hot dogs."

So we stuck weenies on sticks, and held them over the glowing coals, and stuffed ourselves. Everybody was laughing and friendly, even Harold and Lyle. Somebody brought a big bowl of potato salad, and there were pickles and olives and chips, and I kept Susie out of trouble by giving her a bite of something every few minutes. She'd eat anything, even pickles. C. J. sat beside me on the log, and he helped too.

"You have a dog?" I asked him.

He shook his head. "No. Ma says it's too expensive to feed six kids, let alone a dog. Catherine has a bird, but she earns the money for the seed herself, and Ben—he's that one, with the catsup dripping off his chin—has two goldfish."

I hadn't given Susie anything for a few minutes, and she nudged my knee with her square jaw. "You know anything about training dogs?"

"Not really, but I guess you just keep trying. Maybe you could get a book from the bookmobile about it. It comes tomorrow, and then you have to wait a week for them to bring whatever you ordered."

"Would you help me?" I asked. It was the closest I could get to asking if he'd be my friend.

"Sure," C. J. said, nodding.

Walking home later, after the singing and with my belly so full it was uncomfortable, I felt a little better than I had last night.

I supposed I'd get used to C. J.'s face sooner or later, and he was nicer than Harold, whose family was afraid to cross him. And maybe with C. J.'s help I'd be able to teach Susie how to behave a little bit better in the time I had before I could go home.

12

The homesickness didn't go away. But during the days, once I met C. J., there was at least something to do.

He taught me how to fly the dragon kite, and then he showed me how to build one of my own. We spent several days working on it in the Bedrosians' garage.

Sometimes Catherine came out with us onto the beach, and I found out she and C. J. were twins. Sometimes they quarreled with the other kids in their family, but never with each other.

The first time she joined us, she smiled shyly. "Thank you for saving Laurel. I was supposed to be watching her, but she's so quick. When Ben fell and split his lip on a log, and I was trying to stop the bleeding, Laurel just took off. I'd missed her when she started into the surf, but I couldn't have got there in time."

"Me neither," C. J. said gruffly.

To cover my embarrassment, I said, "I might not have made it myself if C. J. hadn't grabbed hold of my collar."

Mrs. Bedrosian was kind of like Mrs. Patton. Not in looks, just in the attitudes she had. She was skinny and dark like her kids, and she never seemed to sit down; she was always hanging out laundry or cooking or putting Band-Aids on one of the kids. We could help ourselves to crackers and peanut butter or big green Granny Smith apples if we got hungry, and sometimes she made cookies. She didn't seem to worry about how much sand anybody tracked in, or how many times we slammed the doors, or if there were wet bathing suits draped over the edge of the bathtub most of the time, or if people came to meals on time or not.

"We usually get there, though," C. J. said, grinning that funny monkey grin that I got used to pretty fast. "With this crew if you're late there might not be anything left to eat."

The bookmobile, which showed up in front of the store every Monday afternoon, had a book about training dogs, so we didn't have to wait. The most important thing, the book said, was patience and then came kindness.

"It's hard," I complained a couple of days later, "to be patient with a dog that's so totally stupid." I stared down at Susie, who was with us on the beach. "Don't you know *anything*?"

Susie joyously responded by lunging into me, knocking me backward, and Catherine laughed.

"She likes you, David."

"She likes everybody. If a burglar ever broke in, she'd probably kiss him to death."

"Let me see the book." I handed it over and watched her as she sat on a log, looking at it. She was a pretty girl. I wondered if C. J. had looked like her before he went through that windshield.

"I'll help you train her," she offered, and I was glad to have the help. "Come here, Susie."

I dragged the dog off before she knocked Catherine over, and together we pushed Susie into position as we told her, over and over, to sit.

After a few days, she got so she'd do it, for a few seconds, but that was all. Then she'd leap up and chase a gull, or dash into the water, or tear after a horse and rider or another dog, whoever was on the beach besides ourselves.

We couldn't get her to stay. We couldn't get her to shake hands or lie down. We couldn't get her to speak for a bite to eat. Instead, she'd jump up and snatch whatever it was out of our hands. If it hadn't been for Catherine, I'd have given up.

"Patience, remember?" she'd say, so we kept trying.

All the Bedrosians were readers. Both Catherine and C. J. read to the younger kids, and I kind of liked sitting and listening too, even to silly stories I'd have felt foolish reading to myself. Like Steven Kellogg's Pinkerton stories, or *The True Story of the Three Little Pigs*, which was a riot.

After the first couple of days, when C. J. was self-conscious and so was I, I didn't even think about his looks anymore. Not unless Harold and Lyle came along.

Harold never missed a chance to snipe at C. J. "Hey, monkey face," he'd say if he met us at the store or the Burger Barrel, or once in a while on the beach. "How you doing?"

C. J. ignored him. When I finally asked why he didn't punch Harold out—I'd learned that he was strong for being so skinny, and he could outwrestle me, so I figured he could deal with tubby Harold—C. J. shrugged.

"Nobody likes the way I look, not even me. So why should I try to fight the world?" He gave me that quick, amused glance I was getting used to. "When I get through with the plastic surgery, I may be better looking than he is, and *I* won't be fat."

Harold was hard to ignore, though. If we turned around and walked away from him, he'd often follow after us, still making remarks.

"How come you want to run around with a monkey?" he asked me once. "You want to come over and play Nintendo again?"

Not if I had to pay for the games again, I thought. "We're busy building kites," I said evenly.

"Only monkeys play with other monkeys," he said. "I bet you hang by your tail from the trees. You got a tail hidden in there?"

He made a grab for my backside, and when I jerked away, he laughed. He sounded like a hyena.

Once or twice, when I met Lyle by himself, he talked all right. But he mentioned C. J. "Doesn't it bother you to look at him?" he said curiously.

"No," I said truthfully, and it was clear he didn't understand how that could be.

On the first day it rained so we couldn't go on the beach or fly the kites, C. J. came over and we read aloud to each other from one of the library books, something by a guy named Frank Peretti, about angels and devils fighting over who was going to control a town. It was pretty good.

At lunchtime, Ruthie served us big bowls of home-made soup and slabs of bread fresh from the oven: she left us alone to eat it while she took something over to old Smiley.

"She's always taking something to somebody," I observed, slathering butter on my chunk of crusty bread.

"Yeah. She's a nice lady," C. J. said. "When Ma was sick last winter, Ruthie came over every day with something to eat so we kids didn't have to try to cook. Catherine and I can make a few things, but they don't taste as good as what Ruthie made. I always wished Ruthie was my grandmother instead of the one I've got."

"You don't like the one you've got?" I asked, thinking about Grandma Elsie and her mauve and cream-colored apartment.

"Not too much. Dad says Grandma Bedrosian made up her mind fifty years ago that she wasn't going to be happy, so she hasn't been. She complains every minute, even when you wait on her hand and foot. Ma says if you're not happy, it's usually your own fault."

Was it, I wondered uneasily? I hadn't been all that happy at home, listening to my folks argue. Sometimes it seemed like I couldn't please them no matter what I did. And except for being glad that C. J. and Catherine were becoming my friends, I wasn't really happy at Ruthie's, either. It was hard to figure how I could wish I was home, when things were so unsatisfactory there.

But the minister had said pretty much the same thing that first Sunday in church. That if you were depressed, you had to do something about it yourself, because the main reason was you were thinking too much about yourself. Being selfish.

"Well, Ruthie seems pretty contented most of the time," I observed.

"Ma says it's because she's always doing things for other people. The old people, the shut-ins. She even tried to do something for Harold's mother, but I guess she gave up. Ma says Mrs. Kevan is probably mentally ill, but not sick enough to lock her up. That's why Harold's such a creep."

At least Mom wasn't mentally ill, I thought. That would be a lot harder to take than just having her be so interested in her career, and so busy selling property, that she didn't have time for me or Dad.

Nobody had any time to think about me, it seemed. I kept expecting Mom to call me, but she didn't. I guess she was too busy, or the times didn't work out right between the different time zones, but I kept hoping.

Dad didn't call, either, at least not right away. And then he didn't call on his own, but because Ruthie called him first.

I wasn't supposed to know about that, of course. I was on the beach with C. J., and I came back to leave my sweatshirt because it was getting too warm. Once I'd just taken it off and hung it over a log, but Susie got hold of it and dragged it way off in the dunes, and we'd had to spend half an hour finding it. It was my best one, and I didn't want her to get at it again.

I figured as long as I'd come back to the house, I'd make a sandwich, so I came in the back door. I had the jelly jar out when I heard Ruthie's voice from the living room.

"I swore I'd mind my own business," she said, "but there are limits, Jerrol."

Dad? Dad was here? I put down the jar and was moving in that direction when I realized she was talking on the phone, not to someone who was in the living room with her.

I stopped, listening without even being aware that I was eavesdropping.

"Neither one of you has so much as sent the boy a postcard since he's been here, nearly two weeks now. He's homesick, son. He needs to know someone cares about him. Well, would it be too much trouble to pick up the phone occasionally and call him if you can't get out here to see him?"

I held my breath, feeling as if there was an elephant on my chest.

Part of me figured he shouldn't have to be reminded he had a kid away from home, while another part was eager to talk to him.

Dad must have said something, because it was quiet for a moment, and then Ruthie said rather sharply, "For heaven's sake, Jerrol, aren't you even communicating with *each other*?"

She could only mean with Mom, I thought, and I tried to fight off a flash of pain.

Ruthie still sounded cross. "Well, regardless of that, you have a son who needs both of you, and he isn't hearing from either one. I don't mind having him here. He's a perfectly nice boy; and outside of eating me out of house and home he doesn't cause any trouble, but it's you and Gail he needs, and you're falling down on your job. He'll be here around suppertime, and I suggest you call him then, about six o'clock. Now I have to go. I promised Pastor Grady I'd look in on Mrs. Sudds while he was away; she fractured her hip last month and mostly the poor soul just sits there all by herself. But you remember you have a child here who's eating his heart out for some word from home."

Dad must have said something else, and then Ruthie said, "Well, good. I hope so," and hung up.

She had sounded quite impatient with him, the way

Mom often did with me. I wondered if all parents talked to their kids that way, even when they were grown-up. I'd never heard Tim's mom, or C. J.'s, either, use that tone on *their* kids, except once when Tim tracked mud in on the rug.

Ruthie left the house then, by the front door, so she didn't know I had been there, hearing her conversation with my dad.

When he called that night, Ruthie was just taking the food out of the oven. "You get it, David," she called, and I picked up the phone.

"Hi, David," Dad's voice said. "I thought it was about time I checked up on you."

Yeah, after Ruthie had reminded him, I thought, but I was glad to hear from him. He said he'd been real busy, and asked what I'd been doing, and I told him. Then I asked if he'd heard from Mom.

"No, I guess she's been pretty busy too," he said, as if it didn't matter.

"But she's coming home in another two weeks, right?" I asked.

"That was the original plan, so I suppose so. Well, take care, son, and do what Ma tells you."

Ruthie hardly ever told me what to do, not like at home where someone was always telling me what to do or not do, but I didn't tell him that. That was probably one reason Mom thought Ruthie wasn't fit to raise a kid.

"Can't you come out and see me next weekend?" I suggested.

"We'll see how it works out, okay?" Dad asked, and I felt a disappointed letdown. I was pretty sure he wouldn't come, especially after he added, "It's an all-day trip out there, you know, even if I only stay for an hour or two."

Talking to him didn't really make me feel much better, I decided, going back to the supper table. I wished I hadn't overheard Ruthie, hadn't known it was *her* idea, not his, to call me.

While we were doing the dishes, I asked Ruthie the question that kept staying on my mind.

"You and Grandpa Frank were married for a long time, weren't you?"

"Forty-two years," she agreed, handing me a plate to wipe.

"Did you ever think about getting a divorce?"

I tried to keep it casual, but she shot me a shrewd glance. "No, not really. There were a couple of times I could cheerfully have murdered him, though."

"Really?"

Ruthie laughed. "Well, almost really. We got along pretty well, though. Most of the time. We had a lot of hard times in the early years, but we worked together. We came through. People don't work as hard to hold a marriage together these days, sometimes, as we did in those days. You worrying about your folks, David?"

"Yes," I admitted quietly.

She rested a hand on my shoulder. "Things will work out," she said, and I wanted to believe her. I didn't know if I did, though. Not after Mom had been gone for two weeks, and she and Dad hadn't even tried to talk to each other yet.

I couldn't help worrying, when I was lying in bed in the dark, about what would happen if my folks didn't make up by the time Mom came home again.

13

Dad didn't come on the weekend. I'd expected that, but I was still disappointed. I did get a postcard from Hawaii, showing a surfer on a big wave, but all Mom said was, "Hi, David. Hope you're having fun with Ruthie."

What did she think a grandmother and a grandson would do for fun in a place like Little Beach? Especially when Ruthie only had Social Security to live on? I knew it wasn't enough to buy very much, and she spent quite a bit of it on food that went to other people.

I remembered she'd told Dad I was eating her out of house and home, and I was worried maybe she couldn't afford to feed me, but when I cut back to one helping of each thing she asked if I were sick.

"Your father always ate like a horse when he was your

age. I hope you're not coming down with something. I'll feel guilty if you don't eat up everything your dad paid me to feed you."

I felt better, knowing Dad was paying her something to buy groceries with. So I had seconds and thirds of everything.

I wondered why Mom had said Ruthie wasn't fit to raise a child. Just because she didn't tell me when to take a bath or go to bed, and fed me tacos or burritos instead of spinach soufflé, and let me read whatever I wanted?

One afternoon C. J. was there, in the little bedroom. I felt self-conscious about inviting him in because I'd been in *his* room. Mine was so empty, more like a storage area, while C. J. shared a room with three brothers, and it was full of all kinds of fascinating stuff. They had bunk beds and the walls were covered with posters and drawings, and there were toys and balls and skates and stuff everywhere.

My copy of the *Evergreen* was lying on the stand beside the bed. It stood out because there was so little else around, except for Officer McGoo, on top of the dresser. C. J. hadn't spotted the teddy bear yet, and I wondered if I could grab it and stuff it under the bed.

C. J. picked up the school magazine and said, "What's this?"

"Uh, it's a magazine my school put together," I said.

He flipped through the pages. "Poems, huh? Hey, here's one you wrote!"

"Yeah," I said, not sure how he'd react to poetry.

He read it through silently, then repeated, "My chest won't let anyone see its feelings or its true self, just like me."

I waited nervously, edging toward Officer McGoo.

C. J. nodded. "I've felt like that. Would you bring this over and show it to my ma?"

"Sure, I guess so."

I'd almost reached McGoo when C. J. suddenly turned around and saw the bear.

"Hey! A cop!"

I was nervous again. The only teddy bear I'd seen at his house was on his youngest brother's bed. "Dad and I were in an accident once, a long time ago. The cop who came told me to hang on to McGoo. I brought him along to just sort of, uh, you know, have something familiar around."

I hoped he didn't think I slept with it.

C. J. picked up the bear and examined the badge up close. "Pretty authentic uniform, isn't it? Even a gun in his holster. I've got an old Smokey the Bear in uniform. It used to play the song about Smokey the Bear when you pulled a string on its back, but the string broke. Catherine's got a bear that's as big as Laurel. She keeps it up high so Laurel can't reach it."

He put McGoo back on the dresser. "Too bad we

don't have a real cop around here to do something about Harold. Ben saw him take some candy bars at the store last night, but Harold called him a liar and said he'd beat him up if he told. Now Ben's afraid to go to the store."

"Harold's a creep," I said, and C. J. nodded.

We found out how much of a creep he was that same afternoon when we headed for the beach. We met Catherine and the small Bedrosians coming home. Ben and Raymond were crying, and Johnnie and Catherine looked angry.

"What's wrong?" C. J. asked.

The words came out of his twin in a spurt. "We spent all morning building a sand fort, and that rotten Harold came along and kicked it all apart just before we got back to it after lunch!"

"Did you see him do it?" C. J. demanded.

"He was walking away laughing," Catherine said. "Why does he have to be so mean?"

We all walked back down to look at the ruins.

"We had a moat and everything," Raymond said. "He kicked it all in."

I could see that C. J. was angry too, and I felt my hands knotting into fists. It was bad enough when Harold picked on C. J., but it was rotten for him to pick on little kids.

"Well," C. J. said, taking Ben's hand, "I guess we'll have to help you rebuild it, won't we, David?"

So we did, and after a while I forgot why we were building this elaborate castle, and just enjoyed kneeling there on the wet sand with the sun on my back and the breeze in my hair.

The little kids got enthusiastic about it, and except for Susie knocking Ben over so he accidentally sat on one corner tower so we had to rebuild it, everything went well until we had one of the best sand castles I'd ever seen.

We knew it would only last until the tide came in again, so the kids went up and got Mrs. Bedrosian to come and look at it before that happened.

"It's even nicer than the one we made first," Raymond told her. He scowled. "But we wanted that one too, and that crummy Harold kicked it all to pieces."

Mrs. Bedrosian sighed. "Poor Harold. He's an unhappy boy, I think. He needs his father, who never comes to see him, and his mother isn't functioning well enough to help him much, either. Try to be nice to him if you can."

I don't think anybody felt like being nice to him. I know *I* didn't.

I almost hoped Harold would come back, and I think C. J. did too. But Harold didn't show, and by the next morning the sea had erased all traces of our masterpiece.

The days were good. The nights were bad.

I hated going to bed in that bedroom that still looked like a storeroom. It wasn't *my* room. Mom didn't call or send any more postcards, and Dad didn't come, and I was worried.

It wasn't fair what parents did to kids. They picked on them or put them down or neglected them or even abandoned them.

I didn't really think mine would abandon me, but what if they separated? What if they asked me which one I wanted to go with? What if I went with one and then the other one never came to visit, like Harold's dad?

I even finally brought up the subject with Ruthie. Mostly we talked while we did dishes, which never took very long.

"I think my parents are having a lot of trouble," I said.

Ruthie wasn't like a lot of grown-ups, who try to smooth things over and pretend nothing's wrong.

"And you're worrying about it," Ruthie said. "I am too, David."

My mouth went dry. "Do you think they'll get a divorce?"

"I certainly hope not. Adults can usually work things out if they're willing to compromise."

But were they? They hadn't called each other since Mom left for Hawaii, nor written any letters, and if Ruthie hadn't prompted Dad to call me, all I'd have heard from the two of them would have been that one postcard.

I tried not to think about it, and mostly during the

days I didn't, at least not much. But at night, when I was alone in that bedroom that still didn't feel like *mine*, I wanted to go home so bad I hurt all over.

The middle of the last week before they were supposed to come and get me, there was a letter for me.

When Ruthie handed it over, I took it eagerly, thinking that for sure it was from my folks, that Mom was coming home and Dad was coming to get me, maybe in time to meet her at the airport.

Only it wasn't from either of them. It was from Tim.

"Dear David," it said. "I hope you're having a good time at the beach. It's sure been lonesome without you. I hope you get home before we have to go." I stopped reading, doing a double take. Go? "My dad has been transferred to Dallas, and Mom wants us to get moved and settled there before school starts. It all depends if Dad can find a house soon enough. Do you suppose you could ever come to visit me in Dallas?"

I couldn't believe it. I couldn't even finish reading the rest of the letter right then. Tim was moving! We'd been friends forever, and we understood each other, and it was okay with his mom if I went over there every day after school.

We'd been best buddies for so long I didn't know how I'd ever get along without him. My eyes burned. Tim was the closest thing I'd ever have to a brother. I guess it wasn't babyish to cry a little at the thought of losing him.

When I finally got up enough nerve to read the whole letter, I darned near cried again when I read the postscript. "Mom said I should box up all your train stuff, and she'd take it over to your apartment. I'm sure going to miss you and playing trains together, David."

C. J. was down too when I talked to him a little later. I didn't realize it right away, only when I'd told him about my best friend moving away and he just nodded soberly.

"Sometimes things are crummy," he said, and I could tell by his face, when I really looked at it, that he had problems of his own.

"What's up with you?" I asked quietly.

He swallowed. "My ma got a letter this morning. They want me to go back in the hospital for another surgery week after next."

"On your face?" I almost hurt, thinking about it.

"Plastic surgery again," C. J. confirmed.

"Was it pretty bad, before?" I could almost feel it myself.

He swallowed again. "Yeah. 'Course I want to have it done, you know. I mean, I don't want to look like this the rest of my life, so people look at me as if I'm a freak. Call me names. Turn around and quick look away because they can't stand to see what I look like."

"That's because they don't know you," I said. "I never even think about how you look anymore."

"Yeah. But the kids in school aren't like that. Nobody

wants to do things with me in school. And every time we go out anywhere, away from Little Beach, people stare at me and make remarks."

I wished I could do something to make it better for him. But I couldn't even make it better for myself.

Some days aren't as good as others.

And some are even worse.

I hadn't been back to Harold's house, and when I met him he often made jeering remarks about my being a monkey because I associated with a monkey. I wasn't as good as C. J. about ignoring him. I hadn't had as much practice.

So when we wound up at the counter in the store at the same time, only three days before Mom's month in Hawaii was supposed to be up, and Harold shot his mouth off again, I didn't just walk away from him as I had before.

"Well, look who's here," he said to Lyle, his constant shadow. "The monkey's tail." He pretended to stumble against me, making me drop the box of crackers Ruthie had sent me to get. Then he giggled when I bent to pick them up, and grabbed the back of my pants like he was going to pull them down. "Let's see your tail, monkey-friend."

I felt the heat in my face as I set the crackers down on the counter. "Why don't you just shut up," I suggested, "and keep your hands to yourself?"

"Oh, I didn't know monkeys could talk, did you, Lyle?"

Lyle's rabbity face smiled. "No, I didn't."

And then it happened.

I didn't like Harold, but I couldn't help feeling sorry for him.

Because his mom came rushing in, out of breath, looking for him. "Harold," she said, not even noticing anyone else in the store. "Come home right now and pack your things."

Harold stared at her. "Pack my things? What're you talking about?"

"We're leaving. I've called for a taxi. We only have an hour and a half to get ready." She started to cry, and even Harold couldn't treat her the way he usually did. Maybe he felt the way I did when my folks were talking about what to do with me.

Harold wet his lips, and he flamed red and then went pale. "What?" he croaked. "You called a *taxi*? To come way out here? What for? What's happened?"

His mother swabbed at her eyes with a handkerchief. "Just because Millie is my sister doesn't give her the right to talk to me the way she did. Even if she is the one who's lived in it the longest, she doesn't really have the right to throw us out of it. It's still partly mine. But I can't stay in the same place with someone who's so . . . so hateful. I'll never forgive her for the things she said."

"Aunt Millie's throwing us out?" Harold asked, disbelieving.

Mrs. Kevan blew her nose and stuffed the hanky in her sweater pocket. "She was very upset about the toad you put in the bread box, Harold. I told her it was just a joke, that you were only a child, but she said you played too many nasty jokes, and that I was a fool for putting up with you, and—"

She broke off, suddenly realizing that everybody in the store was listening to her. "Come on home and pack," she finished.

"But where are we gonna go? Ma, we don't have to let her throw us out—"

"We're leaving. We're going to Aunt Nelly's." She took hold of his shoulder and turned him toward the door.

"But you hate Aunt Nelly! *I* hate Aunt Nelly! Ma, I don't want to leave!"

Usually I guess Mrs. Kevan did pretty much what Harold wanted her to, but it didn't seem that she was going to do that now. She hustled him, still protesting, out of the store.

I drew in a deep breath and took out the money to pay for the crackers. From around the corner of the far aisle, Ben Bedrosian peeked out. There was a little smile on his face.

"Do you think he's really moving out of Little Beach, David?" he asked.

I swallowed. "It sure sounded like it," I agreed.

Part of me was feeling the same thing Ben was: relief that Harold wouldn't be around to pick on everybody anymore.

But deep down inside there was another feeling. I felt sort of sorry for Harold, even if he was a jerk.

14

Ruthie already knew about Harold and Mrs. Kevan's moving by the time I'd run home.

"It doesn't take long for news to get around in this place," Ruthie said. "Poor woman. She's been very disturbed for a very long time, since long before her husband deserted her and Harold. She and Millie have quarreled before, and I think Harold made it harder for both of them to live together in peace."

I spoke slowly. "He'd been making fun of me, and I almost hated him. Then his mother came in and said they had to move away, to go live with someone they don't even like." I swallowed, remembering how I'd felt about coming here to stay with Ruthie. "It was like all the meanness just slid away and he was scared and . . . helpless."

Ruthie shook her head. "One time or another, most

of us feel that way. Caught up in things we can't control. It's especially sad when you're only a child."

"It seems funny to feel sorry for him after all the rotten things he did. He was really mean to C. J."

"Sometimes when people hurt," Ruthie said, getting down bowls to set the table, "they strike out at other people. Innocent people. Maybe that's what Harold did. I'm sure he was badly hurt when his father left."

I went to get the silverware to go with the bowls, smelling the savory soup that was simmering in the big kettle. "What do you think will happen to him, Ruthie? If they have to live with somebody they don't like? Somebody who doesn't like them, either?"

"I don't know. I shouldn't think it will be a very happy time. His mother is so . . . fragile. Millie tried to be kind, but I think it was very difficult for her, taking in her sister and a child like Harold. Pastor Grady's gone right over there, but in some situations the church and the community can't help much. We'll have to wait and see. I'm not sure anyone knows where Harold's father is. He's about the only one who could actually help, but nobody's heard anything from him in years."

She began to fill the soup bowls with a big ladle, and I opened up the box of crackers. Some of them were broken because Harold had knocked the box on the floor, but I just dropped the pieces into my bowl.

My folks had gone away and left me, but not forever. I wondered if they were hurting too because they couldn't get along with each other. I didn't know why. I didn't know if it had anything to do with me or not.

Ruthie sat down and put some of the broken crackers into her soup. "I hope you'll be all right here alone for the afternoon," she said. "I promised Pastor Grady I'd go with him over to Mrs. Moser's to do what we can for her. She had a mild stroke a month ago, and she's just come home from the hospital. Her daughter's there with her, but there's more to do than she can manage by herself right away. Everybody's taking turns helping with the meals and cleaning."

I looked at her. She was just an ordinary woman, not young or rich, not educated, not especially pretty. Not the way Grandma Elsie was.

"You're always doing things for everybody else."

Ruthie smiled a little. "That's why we're here, isn't it? To help each other?" She got up to get the peanut butter for more of the crackers, and I spoke to her back.

"The way you helped my folks, by keeping me. And taking food to people, and picking up their mail if they can't get out, and reading to Smiley because he's too blind to see anything but big print, and even taking in stray dogs like Susie."

Susie heard her name and got up, wagging her tail, to nuzzle my hand. I scratched behind her ear and said thoughtfully, "I guess I'm kind of a stray too in a way."

Ruthie put the peanut butter jar on the table and rested a hand on my shoulder for a minute. "Each of us, at one time or another, is a stray, a lost soul. We hold each other together the best we can. When Grandpa Frank died, practically everybody in Little Beach gathered around to help me grieve, to take care of me until I could take care of myself again. People don't always do that in cities these days, and it's one of the reasons I want to stay here, in a little town like this."

I felt closer to Ruthie. But I was still alone when I thought about home.

Tomorrow, I thought, it would be a month since Mom went away. Tonight probably Dad would call and say he was coming to get me.

But he didn't.

I didn't want to think about Harold, and how his dad had gone off and left the rest of the family. How that must have made him feel. How could you forgive your parent for leaving you alone? How could you believe he'd ever cared about you? And how could you not feel guilty, as if you might have said or done something that would have made a difference, kept him from doing it?

Could I have said or done anything that would have made a difference with my parents? Kept my mom from going away for a month? Made Dad figure out a way to keep me at home with him?

When we didn't hear from him, and he didn't come, I finally had to bring up the subject with Ruthie.

"I thought Dad would have been here by now to take me home. Don't you think we should call him and see?"

"Yes, of course," Ruthie said smoothly, though her eyes were troubled. "Call him this evening, David."

He wasn't home. I finally hung up, and tried not to let my lips quiver. "I'll have to try again later," I said.

"Fine," Ruthie said, giving me a pat on the arm. "Put another chunk of wood in the fire, will you, David?"

I did, liking the heat on my face when I opened the door of the stove, looking into the flames inside. It had sort of become my job, to feed the fire, and I didn't mind. We usually spent the evenings either reading books we got from the bookmobile or watching TV. Ruthie never commented on anything I wanted to read, but she was particular about TV programs. If there was a lot of violence or profanity or anything she thought was not good for me, she told me to turn it off or change channels. "Sets a bad example," she said, so more often than not we just read books.

Ruthie rocked in her chair, and I sat in a corner of the old couch; it didn't look as good as our couch at home, but it was more comfortable, and Ruthie didn't care if I ate while I was sitting there. I was reading a book called *Death Walk*; it was by Walt Morey and I'd read some of his other books, like *Gentle Ben* and *Kavik the Wolf Dog* and liked them a lot. I liked this one too because it was about this kid having some dangerous adventures in Alaska. Only I had trouble concentrating because I kept thinking about Dad.

He still wasn't home when I tried to call again about ten o'clock. Ruthie put aside the paper she was reading. "We'll try again in the morning," she said. "Maybe he had to go out of town."

Maybe he had, because he still didn't answer the phone the next morning. Why hadn't he remembered that it was time to come after me? How could you forget a thing like that?

And then, just before lunchtime, the phone rang. I made a dash for it. "Hello?"

"Hi, son," Dad said, and I felt such a wave of relief that I was practically weak with it.

"Hi, Dad. Are you coming to get me today?"

"Well, no, David. Not yet. Everything's okay there, isn't it?"

Disappointment made me almost sick to my stomach. "Well, I guess, but I want to go home. Is Mom back from Hawaii?"

"Yes." He said it guardedly, and the alarm in my head went off. "We, uh, we've been doing some talking, trying to work some things out."

I sank onto the edge of the nearest chair. "How long's she been home?"

"Day before yesterday," Dad said, and I squeezed the phone so hard my knuckles went white. Day before yesterday, while I sat here worrying and waiting? Why hadn't they called?

"Look, son, let me talk to Grandma, okay?"

For a moment I couldn't move, then I handed the telephone toward Ruthie. "He wants to talk to you." Why not me? I wondered wildly. I was the one he was supposed to come and get.

"Hello, Jerrol," Ruthie said. As she listened, I saw

her kind face get hard and still. "Yes, of course," she said finally, but I knew her well enough by now to know that she was angry. "I think you'd better explain that to David yourself."

She handed the receiver back to me, but she didn't go away. She stood close beside me when I said, "Dad?"

"David, your mother and I are having some difficulties. We think—well, maybe that it would be better for you to stay with Ma just a little bit longer, while we make some decisions."

"What kind of decisions?" I wanted to know. My heart was beating so hard I could hear it in my ears, pounding, pounding.

"About what we're going to do, as a family," Dad said heavily. "I guess you noticed we weren't getting along so well, before your mom left for Hawaii. We have problems."

"About me?" I asked, and then almost wished I hadn't, because I didn't want to hear the answer.

"Certainly some of our decisions will be about you," Dad said immediately. "You're the most important part of our family."

Important, when they'd ignored me for the past four and a half weeks? I wanted to say it, but I couldn't. I couldn't say anything, just wait while the ache in my chest increased.

"It's all right with Ma if you stay there for a few more days. That's all it'll be, then I'll come down and see you."

His words were making me dizzy, sick. See me? Not get me?

The words felt as if they were torn out of my throat. "Is it something I did, my fault? I didn't mean to—"

"No, no, David, nothing's your fault. It's between me and your mother—"

I wanted to say something, but I couldn't. My throat seemed paralyzed.

"Look, son," Dad said, "you just hang in there, and I'll get back to you as soon as I can, okay? Be a good kid."

And then the line went dead.

I couldn't cry, I thought desperately, not in front of Ruthie. And then I looked up and saw that her eyes too were blurred with tears.

She reached out and put her arms around me, hugging me hard, and I hugged back. She wasn't as soft as Mom, and she smelled of fresh-baked bread instead of perfume, and her sweater scratched my cheek.

"I hate him!" I said into Ruthie's chest. "I hate them both!" But inside it felt as if my heart were breaking.

Most grown-ups try to talk you out of hating somebody. Ruthie didn't. She just kept hugging me.

When I could finally talk without choking, I pulled free. "Did he say they're going to get a divorce?"

"No," Ruthie said quietly. "I think they're trying not to." She went into the kitchen and made some cocoa, putting four marshmallows to melt on top of mine. I sat looking at it, wondering if Harold felt any worse tonight than I did, and then I remembered Pastor Grady saying if you were depressed it was likely because you were selfishly thinking of yourself. How could you not think of yourself when you didn't know if you still had a family anymore? Or if your dad left you, or you had to go live with somebody you hated, or somebody died?

My parents weren't dead, but I felt as if they were. I hated them, and grieved for them, all at the same time, and wondered if my life would ever go back to the way it used to be.

How would I survive if it didn't?

15

I wrote a story about a prince whose king and queen parents were so busy doing other things that the prince was left all alone. He didn't care, though. He set off on a quest to find a beautiful princess, and he had to fight his way across a country filled with dragons and giants and evil serpents, slaying them with a wonderful sword. And when he rescued the princess where she had been kept prisoner in her own castle, he married her and lived happily ever after. They never went back to the castle he'd come from, and he never saw his parents again.

C. J. read it and gave me a thoughtful look.

"Now write a story about me," he requested, and I knew he understood the feelings that were having a sort of war inside of me.

"Okay. I'll write about a boy who was turned into an ugly toad, and even though he was a kind and gentle person, nobody liked his looks, so they didn't try to learn to know him. There was a beautiful girl he worshiped from afar, but she wouldn't look at him because he looked like a toad, and she only said, 'Ugh!' at the sight of him."

I glanced at C. J. to see how he was taking it so far. He was watching me with bright eyes, waiting. "And then a traveling plastic surgeon came through town and operated on him and made him incredibly handsome, so she fell madly in love with him," he suggested.

"No," I said. "He found a book in a tower room, and it was full of magic spells, and he tried to do a spell, but he was a klutz. He did a lot of spells and tried to improve various things. To please the princess, he tried to make the roses more beautiful. They were red, but he turned them dark purple, and they smelled like rotten eggs. Every spell went wrong. The seaside had a wide beach with dirty dark sand, but when he tried to make it more pale and beautiful, the shore turned darker and it was lined with black rocks. Then he tried to change the people to make them wise and handsome instead of ordinary, and that didn't work, either. The magic turned them all green, and they were covered with warts."

I paused to see how he was taking this. So far he seemed to be waiting with bated breath, so I went on.

"The people were so upset they complained to the princess. She thought they were right, so she had a fight with the prince, and he got so angry at their ingratitude that he tried to put a spell on *her*."

"And?" C. J. prompted, sitting on the edge of the bed.

"And as usual, it went wrong. Instead of making her lose her voice so she would shut up, it turned her into a toad."

"This is crazy," C. J. said. "I thought this story was supposed to be about *me*."

I ignored that and finished the story. "The prince-turned-toad thought she was the most beautiful toad he had ever seen, and he proposed, and she accepted him. So they were married, and they lived with her green countrymen with the warts, which they decided they liked. And they all lived happily ever after."

C. J. fell backward on the bed with a spurt of laughter. "That's the dumbest story I ever heard!"

"Right," I agreed, and fell on top of him and wrestled him off onto the floor. "Now you tell a better one."

We were sprawled on the linoleum by now. C. J. sat up and looked at me, the laughter slowly running out of him as we stared at each other.

"I wish you didn't have to go home to Everett, David," he said. "I wish you could stay here."

"I wish you could go with me," I said, thinking about Tim moving away to Dallas, leaving me without a best friend.

C. J. slumped against the side of the bed. "I wish I didn't have to go back in the hospital and have another operation on my face. No, I don't, really, because I want my face fixed, but I wish you could be here when I come home."

"How long will you have to be in there?" I asked quietly, all the fun gone out of things.

"Not very long. Probably only a few days, if it's like last time." We had knocked Officer McGoo off the dresser while we were horsing around, and C. J. idly reached over and picked him up. "I hope I won't have to miss any school before it heals enough so the bandages come off. It's bad enough to go back to school when everyone else does, but it's worse if I'm later than the rest of the kids. Everybody will look at me, and some of them will make remarks. And the grown-ups will quick look away."

"Maybe it will work better this time," I suggested. "Maybe you'll look better."

C. J. hugged McGoo. I didn't think he even knew he was doing it. "They already told me it would probably take another six or eight operations. Maybe more."

I drew in a deep breath and stood up. "Come on, let's go down on the beach."

I hadn't understood Ruthie's love for the ocean when I first came here, but I was beginning to. There was something soothing about the sound of the surf that drowned out everything else, about the way the waves rushed in, and broke over your feet if you got too close, and the way it slid back out into the sea. It kept happening over and over, no matter what you did. There was no way to stop it. No more than any way I had to stop anything else. No matter how much anything hurt, life went right on.

I suddenly remembered Ruthie saying, "That's what we're here for, isn't it? To help each other."

Only sometimes there wasn't much you could do to help. Yourself or anybody else.

We slogged through loose sand, up over the dunes, out to the beach, not saying much. Susie tore ahead of us, pausing once in a while to look back, ignoring the commands I gave her automatically from time to time.

She caught sight of a solitary figure out there on the edge of the waves, standing safely above the reach of the riptide. She was off, running full out, leaping on him even as I yelled at her to stop, to come back.

She knocked him staggering off balance, down on one knee. Lyle shoved her off, but he didn't get up, watching us come. Then when we got close he glanced off to the side, as if we weren't there at all.

I wondered if he was remembering all the times he'd been with Harold, when Harold made his hateful remarks, and thinking how we probably felt about him.

Lyle had been kind of a jerk too. But when I went home—if I ever did—he and C. J. would be the only boys anywhere near the same age left in Little Beach.

I walked up close to Lyle and picked up a stick to throw for Susie, to get her away for a minute. "Hi," I said.

"Hi," Lyle said, still kneeling where Susie'd left him.

He glanced at us cautiously, maybe wondering if we were going to gang up on him. He and Harold had done that enough, when there was only one person or a couple of smaller ones to stand up to them.

"We're gonna build a castle," C. J. said. "You want to help?"

Hope leaped into Lyle's face. "Yeah, sure!"

So we made this humongous castle, and stayed on the beach until we got hungry; and when we went to Ruthie's house for something to eat, Lyle came with us. He never said a word about C. J.'s scarred face.

At least when I went home, I thought, C. J. wouldn't be entirely alone.

Though maybe I would.

Four days went by without hearing a word from my parents. I cried at night, once, but the other times I felt angry and frustrated, thinking about them.

Once I said to Ruthie, "Not much in life is fair, is it?" and she said, as if she understood, "Sometimes it seems that way, David."

"Why is there never anything a kid can do?"

She was mending a sock with a light bulb inside it to hold it in position, and she didn't look at me, just kept running the darning needle through the sock. "All you can do is look out for yourself, protect yourself as much as you can. The tricky part is to do that without shutting yourself off from all the good things too. Without becoming hard with a shell that means when something good comes along it can no longer touch you."

I felt confused. I didn't really understand quite how to do that. "So what do I do?"

She did stop stitching then. "I don't know, either, David. We tried to be good parents to your father, and we seldom quarreled and were never apart. He grew up independent and ready to move out when it was time to leave. But even grown-ups don't get past the need to have someone they're close to, someone to lean on, to share with. It's painful when someone you've trusted and relied on goes away. I think your parents are hurting now, just as you are. But being an adult doesn't necessarily mean you know what to do, how to handle big problems. Often we just have to wait and see how they work out."

And what if they worked out wrong? I thought a little later when I went to bed. What if Mom and Dad decided they didn't want to be married to each other any longer? What if I had to choose between them, which one to live with? Or if I had to spend some time with each of them, so there was never any one place that was home? Or, the dread thought crept into the darkness, what if neither of them wanted to be bothered with me?

And finally, when I thought I couldn't bear it any longer, the phone call came. Ruthie told me as soon as I came in.

"Your parents will be here tomorrow," she said. "I don't know what they've decided, but they'll talk to you then."

I felt burning up and icy cold all at the same time. "Are they coming to take me home?"

Her eyes showed that she hurt too on my behalf. "They didn't say, David. Only that they'd talk to you tomorrow."

So there was nothing to do except wait, and worry. And finally that night in bed I knew what I had to do. The idea scared me, and I didn't know if it was the right one. But I hoped I was brave enough to speak out, even though it might not work.

For once they were early, before I was expecting them. I'd stayed at Ruthie's, not going out with C. J. to fly kites. It was a beautiful day to be on the beach. The fog had burned off early, the sea was calm, and the sun was warm in a cloudless sky.

Susie came to nuzzle me as I sat on Ruthie's front steps. Her brown eyes were bright and friendly as she put her face into mine.

"You're a stupid dog," I told her, scratching behind her ears. "You can't learn to sit or stay or speak or get down or anything worthwhile."

Susie wagged her tail and poked me harder with her nose. I leaned my head against her flank, my hands caught in her wiry fur. "You aren't the kind of dog I wanted at all," I told her in a muffled voice. "I wanted a puppy, a soft, smart one."

She whined. I wondered how much she understood of what I said. She knew I needed comfort, though, and leaned against me so hard she finally made me laugh, because she pushed me right off the step into the sand.

And then, suddenly, Mom and Dad were there, pulling up at the front of the house. I wondered how he'd talked her into getting up early enough to get here before midafternoon.

Ruthie came out, wiping her hands on a dish towel. She was wearing the same colorless old pants she'd had on the day I came, and that dark red sweatshirt that said DON'T ASK ME, I DON'T KNOW.

They got out of the car and came toward us. Mom was wearing dark glasses with white frames, and white slacks and sandals with a bright flowered shirt. She'd gotten tanned in Hawaii.

Dad came toward us more slowly. I looked at him carefully, my heart hammering inside my chest, but I couldn't tell what he was thinking.

They stopped a few feet away. "Hi, honey," Mom said, but she didn't reach out to hug me, and I didn't run to hug her, either. "Hello, Ruthie." Mom smiled at her, but we couldn't see her eyes behind the dark glasses. They made me feel as if she were a stranger, almost.

"Hello, Gail." There was nothing to give Ruthie's feelings away, either. "David's been waiting for you." She hesitated, then added, "To take him home. Are you going to take him home?"

There was a short silence. I didn't think Mom liked being put on the defensive that way.

Dad cleared his throat. "Yes, we've come to get him," he said. "Only we . . . well, we need to talk to him a little bit first. To explain to him how things are."

My insides felt like jelly. I couldn't say anything, but I was glad Ruthie did.

"How *are* things, Jerrol?"

Mom spoke before Dad could. "We're having a difficult time right now. I'm sure you guessed that. In our marriage, our careers. Neither of us is exactly sure how it's going to turn out, but we're trying to come to a mutual agreement."

But that's what they'd been supposed to be doing, ever since Mom got back from Hawaii, I thought. She'd been home a week now. How much time did they need to figure it out?

"We don't think we want to give up our apartment right now," Dad explained, "because it's a nice one, and we had trouble finding it in the first place. But Gail and I aren't . . . comfortable, being together there at the moment. We're considering a trial separation, seeing each other but not living together for a time. Maybe that way we can clarify a few matters—"

My heart had sunk, but I knew I couldn't just let it lie there at the bottom of my stomach.

"We thought we'd take David home—," Mom said, and then stopped in midsentence when I interrupted.

"No."

"No?" Dad echoed.

"It's not fair," I said as steadily as I could. "Not unless it's my fault that you . . . can't live together."

There was a chorus of protest from both throats. "No, David, of course it's not your fault—"

My legs were shaky, and I was glad Susie was pushing up hard against me. I looked at Ruthie, who had come out to stand beside me, then back at my folks.

"I missed you something awful when you left me here," I told them. "I didn't really know Ruthie, or Susie, or anyone else here. You didn't seem to care very much. You didn't call me or write to me or anything."

Remembering made my throat ache, but I kept on, not letting them interrupt. Mom started to speak, but Dad put a hand on her shoulder and made her stop.

"I heard you that night you were fighting. The night you said 'What are we going to do about David?' and it was like you had to decide to put a dog in a kennel while you went away and did whatever it was you each wanted to do. You didn't even worry about if the kennel was the best place. You didn't ask me what I thought. It didn't even matter to you that I was scared and homesick—"

"David—," Mom said, taking off her glasses and moving toward me.

I stepped closer to Ruthie and felt her hand settle on my shoulder. My voice cracked, but I didn't stop saying those things I had thought about last night, lying there alone in the dark.

"I don't want to do that again," I said. "Go home and listen to you argue, and wait for when you wonder again what you're going to do with me. Ruthie . . . Ruthie's more caring about Susie and the neighbors, old Smiley and the Bedrosians and even Harold's crazy mother, and she's not even related to any of them."

Mom got white under her tan, and she started to speak again, but Dad stopped her once more.

I could feel Ruthie, strong and still beside me. I twisted to look up at her, and she wasn't much taller than I was.

"I know this was only a visit, Ruthie, because they didn't want me around for a while. If it was my fault or not, they didn't really want me. And now they don't know if they want each other or not."

My voice broke again, but I was feeling stubborn now, determined to say it all, because next time I might not have Ruthie there to be on my side, or stupid old Susie leaning against my leg. I wasn't sure I'd be brave enough without them. It was now or never.

"It's not fair," I said as strongly as I could. "It's too much to ask me to be around while you decide if we're still a family or not. We—we became a family, Ruthie and Susie and I and everybody who lives here. This house isn't fancy like our apartment at home, but everyone's welcome here. I can track in sand or wet jeans, and have friends over, and . . . and—"

I hated the way my voice went all quavery. Mom said, "Honey," and reached for me, but I stepped backward.

I didn't answer her. I looked at Ruthie. "It was a visit, but maybe this could be a better home than if I went back to Everett. At least until Mom and Dad can make up their minds. Could it, Ruthie? Could it be a home?"

·

I saw the tears spring to her eyes, only inches away from mine, and she turned and gave me a hug.

"Of course it could, David," she said.

That wasn't the end of it, of course. For a while I thought they'd just throw me bodily in the backseat and pack my stuff in around me and take me home, no matter what I thought.

Mom glared at Ruthie and demanded, "Was this your idea?"

I felt Ruthie stiffen, and I knew right then that she didn't like Mom very much. "No, Gail," she said evenly. "It wasn't."

"He's just a little boy," Mom said, pink spots in her cheeks. "He wouldn't have thought of anything like this by himself."

"Weren't you paying attention to what he said?" Ruthie asked. "How he listened to you talking about how to dispose of him when it was inconvenient for you to have him? No different than if you were putting a dog in a kennel?"

Mom had a lot more to say, Dad said a little, and Ruthie didn't say anything but kept her arm around my shoulders so I didn't run out of courage.

"Maybe Ma and I had better discuss this," Dad said finally, and Mom refused to be left out, so they went in the house and sat there talking for quite a while. I didn't try to listen.

Lunchtime came and went, but nobody mentioned

food. I thought if I ate anything, I'd probably throw up. They went on talking and talking, while I sat on the front steps with Susie. She knew there was something wrong, and she put her face right into mine and wagged her tail whenever I looked straight at her or spoke to her.

"I love you, you goofy dog," I said.

Finally they came out of the house. Mom had been crying and her face was all blotchy, and she'd put the sunglasses back on to cover her eyes. I wondered if she had cried about the way I felt, or just because for once she wasn't having her own way.

I stood up, and Dad put a hand on my shoulder. He sounded choked when he said, "All right, David. We're going to try it your way for now."

Neither one of them kissed me good-bye, which was a good thing. I was having trouble holding things together. They got in the car and drove away without me.

I cried while I watched them go, after they couldn't see me anymore. I knew I'd go on being homesick, probably for a long time. And I didn't know for sure if they'd ever come back and get me for keeps, though I hoped some day it might work out that way. I didn't suppose I'd ever stop missing them in a way that was different from the way I missed Tim, or would miss the Bedrosians and Ruthie if I left *them*. There's something special about parents, even if they're not being very nice to you. You need to have them care about you, and I wasn't sure how much mine did.

Catherine and C. J. came over after my parents had

gone. They'd been watching through the curtains at their place. They didn't say anything about the way my eyes were red or my face was wet until I wiped it on my sleeve.

"You staying until I come out of the hospital?" C. J. asked.

"I guess so," I agreed. "I may even get to go to school with you on the bus."

For some reason Susie reached out and nipped my hand. It was a thing she did when she wanted attention.

"Stop it, Susie! Behave yourself," I scolded, glad to have something happen to break the tension. "Sit!"

And to my astonishment, she plunked her butt right down on the sand and wagged her tail, looking up expectantly.

"She sat!" Catherine exclaimed. "David, she minded!"

I moved away from the dog, keeping an eye on her. "Stay, Susie," I told her.

Susie jumped up and came rushing to leap on me, so I leaned against the front of the house to keep from falling.

"Oh, well," Catherine said. "I guess it was too much for her to learn all at once."

"We'll have to keep working on her," I said in disgust.

"Like for the rest of her life," C. J. added, grinning.

"Patience," I said, nodding. "It'll take lots of patience."

I had a sudden realization that everything about my future was going to take lots of patience, and maybe even more courage than it had taken to say the things I'd said to my parents today. But along with the pain inside me that wouldn't go away, that I knew would haunt me in the nights maybe forever, there was a tiny knot of hope.

I would help C. J., and he would help me. So would Catherine and Ruthie and even silly old Susie, whether she knew it or not.

I didn't want to let them see me cry again, right face-to-face. I broke into a run. "Come on, let's go fly kites," I yelled.

We ran toward the beach, Susie tripping us before surging on ahead, feeling the salt air on our faces.